MURDER ACROSS THE MAP

Murder Across The Map

Edited by

Cindy Daniel

Top Publications, Ltd.
Dallas, Texas

Murder Across The Map

A Top Publications Paperback

First Edition

Top Publications, Ltd. Co.
12221 Merit Drive, Suite 950
Dallas, Texas 75251

Foreword

We all know women working together can do wonders and that is exactly what Cindy Daniel and her fellow members of the Sisters in Crime Internet Chapter provide in this wonderful anthology of short stories.

In this collection of stories, the offerings run the gamut from light and cheerful to somber and heartbreaking.

The SINC Internet Chapter hoped to provide a stage for experienced authors as well as introduce new writers and that dream has been achieved.

These stories illuminate fresh visions in a delightful departure from the usual and commonplace.

MURDER ACROSS THE MAP will thrill discriminating readers who seek the unexpected and the original.

Carolyn Hart, May 2005

Acknowledgments

In 2004, when I was President of the Internet Chapter of Sisters In Crime, one of my goals was to find a way to 'give back' to the organization that helped me become a better writer. But, how do you repay those who've given their time, their encouragement, and their unfailing friendship? The answer was two-fold....

You do it by giving authors (new and experienced, members and non-members) an opportunity to showcase their work, and you donate the royalties to the chapter so it can continue the world-wide mission of offering networking, advice and support to mystery authors.

Of course, this isn't a new idea – it's just new to us.

For several authors this anthology lets them realize their dream of being published, for others it is a worthy addition to their printed works. However, for all of us, it is something we know we couldn't have accomplished without the help of a lot of people, and we'd like to thank them:

2005 SINC-IC President, Denise Dietz and the SINC-IC Board of Directors, 2005 SINC National President – Patricia Sprinkle, Jan Christensen, Beth Anderson, Kathy Phillips, Donna Andrews, Beverle Myers, Ann Cavan, and Claire Goldsmith.

A special thanks to Carolyn Hart for her gracious contribution to our anthology and to women mystery writers.

And, to Lonnie Cruse, our copy-editor extraordinaire, you have our heartfelt thanks for your hours and hours of checking our grammar, correcting our em-dashes, and deleting all those pesky semicolons we kept adding. You are not only a fantastic copy-editor and a wonderful author, but a true friend, and we appreciate you!

Cindy Daniel
Editor

Contributing Authors

OUT OF BOUNDS
J.K. Cummins

HOW TO KILL A PEANUT QUEEN
J.M.M. Holloway

LETTERS FROM IRAQ
Kadi Easley

TEN THOUSAND ACRES
Megan Powell

LOVE IS A FOUR LETTER WORD
Pam McWilliams

DEATH IN THE GARDENS
Roberta Rogow

THE BURRO
Heather Hiestand

DEADLY DESSOUS (*DEADLY LINGERIE*)
Gesine Schulz
(Translated by Gunhild Muschenheim)

THE GOOD OLD DAYS
Paul D. Marks

FLOATERS
Patricia Gulley

DEATH BY TRIAL AND ERROR
R. Barri Flowers

A DESOLATE DEATH
Cindy Daniel

STORY ONE

OUT OF BOUNDS
by J.K. Cummins

In a nearby bedroom a woman screamed; a terrified, going-over-the-edge-of-a-cliff kind of scream. William Boyd Jr. knew it was probably just another nightmare in this place of murdered sleep, but it still sent a chill down his spine, like fingernails on a blackboard.

Most of the women managed to keep their demons at bay in the daylight, but nighttime tested their souls. He looked up from his keyboard and listened in case there was anything he needed to do.

Silence.

The knowledge that Doris Chumley would handle any problem comforted him. The resident house-mother was more than Boyd's right arm, she was both legs as well. Unlike him, Doris did understand what they were going through, had been there herself. Not much older than many of the residents, she still called them all 'girls.'

Boyd went back to his computer to work on next year's budget, but five minutes later snap, crackle, pop went the power. Lights, computer, and air-conditioner instantly shut down.

For the past three days, a hurricane pummeled the coast of Baja bringing tropical storms to San Diego, and when heat and humidity put too much pressure on the system, the whole county suffered rolling blackouts.

With his office fast becoming a sauna, Boyd got up from his desk to open the window. The night air, as suffocating as a wet wool blanket, was thick with the threat of rain. In the foothills the show had started: lightning flickering in clouds, thunder rumbling ominously. A real Dr. Frankenstein kind of night. When the door to his office creaked open and a candle moved toward him, he playfully asked, "Igor, is that you?"

"Don't be silly, Mr. Boyd, it's just Doris," she said. "But it is a dark and stormy night."

"I came by to say I gave the girls candles in case the power is off for long," she explained. "Some of them are scared of the dark."

"I know." Boyd had heard the residents' stories but still couldn't imagine what such a life must be like, a life haunted by pain and fear.

Haven House had been built ten years earlier as a refuge for these battered women, thanks to the generosity of the late Melanie Swenson. And when Boyd finished his degree in social services at San Diego State, he'd been hired by her husband to take over its management.

Before leaving, Doris lit another candle and put it on his desk.

Too restless to sit twiddling his thumbs until the power came back on, Boyd loosened his tie and rolled up his sleeves, then picked up the putter and ball he kept next to the filing cabinet. He dumped out the pencil holder to use as a cup and put it on the floor with the candle next to it.

Lightning flashed and a second later a clap of

thunder sounded from the direction of the golf course. Boyd walked back to the window.

Haven House was separated from Shadow Creek Country Club by the stream that was its namesake. Some male members had protested a women's shelter being built so close to a former bastion of the Old Boys, but the times they are a-changin' and one Haven House resident even earned pin money finding lost balls.

Rain began pelting the tin roof of the shed beneath his window. As the moon edged out from behind a cloud, Boyd could make out the dark ribbon of the creek, running high now. After the hard clay soil absorbed all the rain it could take, the creek became a fast-moving stream churning up chunks of mud before it joined the Arroyo River and turned into a raging torrent that rushed down the hill to the Pacific Ocean.

Boyd went back to practice his putting. Off by miles, the ball rolled into a dark corner, and he had to take the candle with him to locate it. He addressed the ball again, repeating a lesson the golf pro at the club had hammered into him: "Don't over-think, let your instincts guide you." The ball went in the cup five times in a row.

Deciding to quit while he was ahead, Boyd sat back down in his big leather chair and put the candle on his desk, illuminating an 8x10 photograph taken in 1992 — Stan Swenson presenting him with the Shadow Creek Country Club's Junior Golf trophy while his proud father and family friend Chet Bennett looked on.

Omigawd.

Cold sweat broke out along Boyd's hairline and

his mouth went dry. The jagged scar like a lightning bolt on Swenson's bare forearm...it was so clear, why hadn't he ever noticed it before?

The weather—hot and sultry as a Louisiana bayou—the same as on that day ten years ago, must have unleashed his unconscious and triggered the epiphany. He was faced with the fact that this place of hope and mercy might have been built on murder.

Few had dared play golf that day because a tropical storm was threatening. They hadn't started until noon because Stan had to work, and by then the course was nearly deserted. Waiting on number five for the group ahead to take their second shots, they leaned against their golf carts, nervously watching black thunderheads massing along the foothills. Wind gusts whipped the tops of the eucalyptus trees and canyon oaks that lined the fairway.

Wiping his sweaty face with a golf towel, Chet looked up at the leaden clouds scudding over head and said, "A man could get himself killed on a day like this."

"Maybe wet, but not killed," said sixteen-year-old William Boyd II, known to everybody as Junior. Stan Swenson — whose Shadow Creek Country Club membership they were playing on — had let Junior fill in to make a foursome. He was the best player on the Mountain View High School golf team, but this was his first time on a private course, and he really wanted to finish the round. "PGA golfers play in the rain all the time," he said hopefully.

"But not if there's lightning." William "Billy" Boyd gave his son an affectionate squeeze on the shoulder. "See that dead oak over there, cleaved right down the middle?" Junior nodded.

"Spare me," Stan said. "That story's older'n dirt, and just about as interesting."

He walked a few feet away to take practice swings. Although he'd never say it, Junior thought that Mr. Swenson was a foul-mouthed blow-hard, and his egg-yolk yellow golf shirt and plaid trousers made him look like a fat banana.

Chet picked up the story. "Anyway, some thirty years ago or so, a golfer took shelter from a storm under that tree. The poor guy was holding onto his five-iron when the lightning hit him. His partners found him dead—the club welded to his hand."

Junior grimaced, and his dad said, "Of course, that was just a freak occurrence. Except for these tropical storms, we don't get much lightning in San Diego."

Stan returned to catch the tail-end of the story. "That may be true, but you never know when lightning's gonna strike." Making the sign of Zorro with the end of his driver on Junior's chest, he said, "Zig, zag, zot-you're dead. But if you gotta go, you gotta go, and what better place than a golf course?"

"Yeah." Chet grinned his pulling-your-leg grin and said, "Don't let anybody ever tell you, Junior, that golf's not a dangerous game."

"Dangerous, smangerous," Stan said, glaring at the three-some up ahead, still not on the green after several wild shots into the long kikuyu grass. "If them sorry asses up there don't finish the god-damned hole pretty soon, I'm gonna hit me a long drive off the tee. Serve 'em right if one of 'em got clobbered."

Junior saw his dad wince and knew he hated cursing, never, ever allowed it around his kids, knew he hated violent talk almost as bad. So he was expecting his father to say something to Stan and was surprised when he didn't.

"Hey, Stick," Stan said, laughing his stupid donkey laugh and prodding Junior in the chest with his finger, "Why don't you go over and get us some beer?"

"Don't be a fool; you know the boy's only sixteen." Junior's dad's eyes were squinty, like they always were when he got mad, and Junior hoped he was going to tell Mr. Swenson to stop calling him 'Stick,' but he didn't.

Stan's face went red, and he pressed his thick lips tight together. For a minute, Junior was afraid he might whack his dad with the driver, but instead he waved the club at Chet, saying, "Then, you go get the beer, Chrome-Dome."

Without a word, the big man took off for the beer cart.

When Junior first took up golf, his dad had told him, "Golf's a gentleman's game, where people are polite and sportsman-like and always follow the rules, even when nobody is watching." But Stan Swenson wasn't a gentleman, and somebody ought to stand up to him.

Chet came back with the beer. After filling the cooler, he handed them around.

While the men sat in the golf carts drinking, Junior swung his club at a dandelion and watched the threatening clouds piling up. At least the three-some up ahead were finally on the green, so maybe they would be able to finish before the storm hit. Trying to hurry his partners, Junior called, "Who's up?"

"Me, of course," Stan said. "Ain't I won the last

four holes?" His smirk took them all in. "I'm gonna have to get me some real competition next time I play-like some spastic Girl Scouts." After a couple more swallows, he dropped his beer can on the ground and walked over to the ball-washer.

Junior picked the can up and tossed it in the trash, then sat down next to his dad. "Is Stan always such a jerk, or is he just feeling bad about his wife dying and all?"

Chet leaned over to clean dirt out of his cleats with a golf tee and said real quiet, "Stan feeling bad? When hell freezes over. The bastard's out here playing golf only a day after his wife's funeral."

"Stan never was one for sentiment," Junior's dad said, shaking his head. "And he can't be too unhappy Melanie died before she was able to spend what was left of her inheritance to build that women's shelter."

"That really must have given the old boy a scare." Chet looked to see if Stan was listening, then continued, "I heard his contracting business was on the ropes — close to bankruptcy — and that Melanie refused to bail him out."

"Now he's got her money and the insurance settlement too."

Before Junior could ask about the settlement, Stan turned and called, "What're you old pussies yammering about?"

"About Melanie's funeral." Chet cleared his throat. "Surprising that Dan didn't turn up to pay his respects...him being so stuck on her all those years and everything."

Stan clutched the golf ball he'd just finished

washing until his knuckles turned white. "Even if I knew where that bastard twin of mine was, do you think I'd invite him to the funeral?" He took a deep breath and watched a red-tailed hawk circling high above the gully before saying, "Dan was always trying to come between Melanie and me, always trying to make her unhappy with her life."

Junior saw his dad and Chet share a look, but neither of them said anything.

The group up ahead was back in their carts, so Stan teed up, took a practice swing, then drove straight down the fairway a couple hundred yards. He walked back and said, "What'd we say, fellas? Ten bucks a hole?"

"Don't be a jackass," Chet said, then walked over to the tee. He topped the ball, and drove it only a few yards into the short rough on the right.

"Guess we're gonna have to get you a club head big as a croquet mallet." Stan gave his hee-haw laugh.

Junior was up next, and his drive went a few yards further than Stan's but landed in a bunker.

"What'd you expect, kid, learning to play from your dad."

After a half-hearted practice swing, Junior's dad teed off. His shot lofted high into the air but landed only about fifty yards down the fairway. He picked up his tee and pocketed it without a word.

Stan shook his head in disbelief. "Damn shame, Billy. This is a long par four, so you can practice your walking." On the way to their carts he said, "I'm gonna take the kid with me. He'll need some pointers on the hole from hell."

"Thanks anyway, I'll ride with my dad."

"Who's Stan to be giving advice?" Junior's dad said as they started up the cart path. "That sorry bastard's been slicing his second shot into the trees or the gully for the past twenty years on this hole. Dollars to donuts, he'll do the same damn thing again today. And if we're lucky, this time the worthless son-of-a-bitch will get himself good and lost, looking for his fucking ball."

The way his dad was cursing made Junior nervous, but he decided to ask, "That ravine looks pretty wild—why would Stan even go searching for his ball down there?"

"Stubborn, that's why. He's as mule-headed as his old man was. Stan never believes there's any lie so bad he can't get out of it." Junior's dad braked the cart hard, then got out. Using a seven-iron, he took a tremendous swing and drove his ball long and straight. Before Junior had a chance to congratulate him on the shot, his dad continued, "Now, his twin brother Dan took after their mom - quiet and considerate. Hard to believe identical twins could be so different."

"I thought if twins looked alike, they'd act alike."

"No way." His dad rubbed his chin and stared at the treetops. "Stan isn't just stubborn, like his dad, he has his rotten temper too. Once, a gang of us were playing baseball in the vacant lot behind Farley's Hardware store. Dan was catching for the opposing team when Stan tried to steal home. Dan tagged him out, and Stan was so mad, he gave his brother a shove that knocked him flat. Dan gashed his arm on a broken bottle. Holding his bleeding arm, he got up and said, 'When you're out, you're out, Stan. You just gotta be a good sport and take it.'"

"Wow."

"Anyway, their father was too cheap to spend money on a doctor, so there were no stitches. But we kids used to think Dan's scar looked kinda neat — sort of like a jagged bolt of lightning."

"He could have been a Chargers Mascot."

Junior's dad laughed, and they drove up to where Chet had just hit a beautiful eight-iron shot to within a few yards of the green. "Good one, you'll make par for sure from there," his dad said, then looked around. "Where's old Stan?"

"He took our cart on up to his ball."

"Jump in, Chet, and we'll give you a lift." The three of them scrunched together and continued up the hill as the sky grew darker by the minute.

"Looks like we're in for it now," Junior's dad said when a few fat raindrops fell on the cart.

"I don't much mind as long as there's no lightning," Chet said. "The damn sky's been threatening so long, the rain might help clear the air."

They pulled up next to Stan's cart, and Junior grabbed a sand wedge and walked over to the bunker to take his shot. With a sharp blow that sent sand flying, he managed to drop his ball on the front of the green. He came back, grinning from ear to ear.

"A chance for a birdie," Chet said, "if your putting's any good."

Bill clapped his son on the back. "Not too shabby, considering your old man was your teacher. You didn't need any tips from Stan after all." He looked around and said, "We've got a twosome waiting behind us, I wonder where Stan's got to."

"He must have sliced his second ball down into the gully," Chet said. "And you know Stan, even if it went as far as the creek, he won't just take the penalty." "Remember how after he and Melanie were first married, Stan paid his brother to caddy for him?" Chet nodded and reached in the cooler for a beer. "And how every time Stan drove into that ravine, he'd send his poor brother traipsing through the bushes and nettles looking for the damn ball."

Chet passed him a bag of pretzels and added, "There was one time, Junior, he even made Dan wade into the creek after it. You know, I think that was the last time the two brothers were ever together. Dan finally got so fed up with the way Stan was treating Melanie that he left town."

"Was Dan in love with Melanie?" Junior asked.

"Yes siree, that boy was crazy about her ever since ninth grade, just like I was about your mom. Melanie would have been happier married to Dan, but his pushy twin won out. I guess that brutish type appeals to some women."

"Brutish?" Chet sat down in the cart. "A wife-beater is closer to the truth. My Eloise heard from a neighbor of theirs that the police were called up to the Swenson's for domestic disputes more than once."

Lightning flashed along the ridge. Junior counted to five before the thunder cracked. "It looks like the storm's at least a mile away, so can we keep on playing?"

But his dad didn't hear him, he was scratching the back of his neck like he always did when he was thinking hard. "You know, Stan had to have an infusion of cash to bail out his business - may have felt like his back was to the wall when Melanie wouldn't give it to him. Makes you wonder if her death was accidental. Was her fall really caused by inadequate slip-proofing on the bottom of that Hilton Hotel bathtub?"

"Well, Stan's lawyer must have convinced the Medical Examiner and the insurance company it was an accident."

"If you ask me, it was more like nobody could prove it wasn't an accident."

Chet frowned and shook his head. "So the bastard'll get away with it."

Junior had kept quiet, afraid they'd stop talking if they remembered he was there, but now he said, "You mean Mr. Swenson murdered his wife?"

Neither one answered him — they just looked hard at each other. Finally Chet said, "Could be he didn't plan it to happen. Maybe they'd been arguing about something, and Stan was mad. Maybe Melanie started to climb in the tub, and he gave her a shove like he did his brother at the baseball game. Who knows?"

Junior stared at his father in disbelief. "Can't you do something?"

His dad shrugged, then looked down, like he was trying to find the answer on the toe of his golf shoe. "What, son? The Las Vegas police closed the case; decided it was an accident. Maybe it was." Thunder rumbled in the distance, and he turned around. "That twosome behind us is getting impatient. I think we should let them play through."

Chet started his cart. "My ball's only a few yards from the green. I say, screw Stan, let's finish the hole before the storm hits."

"I don't like Mr. Swenson much either," Junior said, "but I think we'd better try to find him before we go on playing."

"I guess you're right," his dad agreed. "The ravine's pretty steep in places — he might have broken his leg or something."

Junior volunteered to look, and he was halfway to the junipers that fronted the gully when Chet gave a shout, "Speak of the devil...there he is."

Emerging from behind a big canyon oak was Stan, his seven-iron tucked under his arm. His yellow golf shirt was covered with smudges, and his plaid pants were caked with dirt. He must have taken quite a fall because he was limping. Junior ran over and offered his arm. Smiling weakly, Stan took it and said, "Thanks."

Chet helped him into the golf cart. "What the hell happened, Swenson? You look like you've been wrestling with Beelzebub himself."

"I did. Devil of a hole, always gives me problems." He was breathing hard and wiping dried saliva from the corners of his mouth. "You guys have anything to drink?"

"Nah. We drank it all waiting for you." His dad pursed his lips and shook his head, then said, "You never learn do you? Why didn't you just take your penalty?"

"Sorry. I got carried away." Stan was searching through his pockets.

"Looking for your wallet?" Chet asked.

Closing his eyes, Stan nodded wearily, then leaned his elbows on the front dash of the cart and buried his face in his hands.

"Don't you remember? You always keep it in the

side pocket of your golf bag," Chet said, motioning for Junior to retrieve it.

"Would you mind running back to the drink cart, young fellow?" Swenson pulled out a twenty and handed it to him. "Get us a couple six-packs of Coke."

Junior set off, thinking Mr. Swenson must have had a close call down at the creek because his disposition sure had improved. When he got back with the drinks, no one was talking, but Junior saw messages going back and forth between his dad and Chet, like when his parents were trying to keep something from him and his sister.

Stan was opening his Coke when Chet said, "That wasn't like you at all."

"Excuse me?"

"What Chet means is...." Junior's dad's eyes held Mr. Swenson's. "It wasn't like you to apologize, and it wasn't like you to offer to buy the drinks."

Chet added, "The old Stan never apologized, never paid his fair share."

"Oh, yes, I see what you mean," Swenson said, brushing at the dirt on his pants. "I guess I'd better remember that."

Junior's dad pulled a flask out of his bag and raised it like he was giving a toast. "Sometimes a lie is so bad that you can't get out of it no matter how hard you try. In the end, you have to take the penalty."

"Hear, hear," Chet said, then took the flask and had a swig.

Junior couldn't figure out what was going on, but it felt serious - important.

"I've made a decision," Swenson said, looking at each of them in turn. "Next week, I'm going to request bids for the construction of that women's shelter Melanie wanted built. When it's completed, I'd like to invite all of you — my true and supportive friends — to the dedication ceremony." He took the flask from Chet and raised it again. "To our dear, sweet Melanie, may she now rest in peace."

Junior's dad caught him staring at the jagged scar running like a lightning bolt down Mr. Swenson's arm. Taking the flask, his dad handed it to him, saying, "Have a drink for Melanie, son, and for justice."

Junior took a drink. The whiskey burned his throat and made his eyes water.

A flash of lightning and a clap of thunder, nearer now, made them all jump.

"I think it's time to call it quits," Chet said. "I've had all the golf I can take."

"Yep, about enough," Junior's dad agreed. "We don't want to chance staying out here and getting struck by lightning or something."

Huge drops began to pelt the fairway. Soon, torrents of rain would wash mud down the sides of the gully. The rain and mud would send any debris in the creek rushing down the hillside, away from the golf course and into the Arroyo River. Eventually, everything would be carried all the way to the Pacific Ocean.

Boyd paced his office in the dark, tapping the putter ahead of him like a blind man's cane. Should he call the police? But what proof did he have after all this time? A jagged scar as evidence of a conspiracy to cover up murder? And what good would it do?

Shouldn't justice be par for the course? He dropped the ball and club in the corner and went back to his desk.

The lights came on, and a burst of cool air hit the back of his neck. Staring at the smiling foursome in the photograph, he picked up the phone to call the police. Rules were rules.

But after pushing "9" and "1" he paused to consider. Would it upset the universe if someone went out of bounds, then put a new ball in play without taking his penalty?

Maybe not. Boyd slid the photo under a stack of papers in the bottom drawer and hung up the phone.

STORY TWO

HOW TO KILL A PEANUT QUEEN
by J.M.M. Holloway

Angelique had a bronze casket with silver fittings and a silk lining. A beautician came all the way from Dallas to fix her hair and makeup, if you can imagine. For her final ensemble, she wore royal purple satin brocade and a crystal tiara. Across her chest, a cream-colored sash spelled out her title in gold. The only thing that surprised me was the service being held in Wichita Falls, an hour's drive from home, but then her husband said he wanted the best. Everything must be fit for the queen Angelique was.

At the funeral, I followed Lisa Miller, a dear friend and member of my Sunday school class, to the front to pay respects. "She shouldn't be wearing that tacky ribbon," Lisa said.

"Shush," I said, but Lisa ignored me.

"You don't suppose they'll bury her with that on, do you?" She pointed to a diamond brooch, in the shape of a peanut, pinned to Angelique's dress. "Makes my poor heart flutter to think of such a thing. Everybody knows you should never bury jewelry with a person. Not unless you want some thief to dig it up along with the departed. Why I heard about a woman the next county over who was buried wearing cubic zirconia studs."

While she talked, I led the way back toward our pew, noticing as I went how grand the chapel was. The sun cast bright colors through stained glass windows. Gold edged everything. Rich burgundy carpets hushed our steps. Urns overflowed with lovely floral tributes, but their scent plus the heavy perfume and aftershave in the room made it hard for a person to breathe.

Lisa interrupted herself and rubbed her sternum. "I wouldn't have come if I'd known it would be so close in here."

She had a minor heart ailment, one she often made too much of, but now she actually did look faint.

Always looking out for the other person, I said, "We'd better get you outside."

A few minutes later the pallbearers emerged with their burden, followed by Angelique's widowed husband, Ray. As he watched the casket disappear into the hearse, he broke down in sobs. My heart went out to him. In spite of all the talk it was bound to cause, I just had to go over and hug his neck. Soon as I did, he got worse, weeping like a woman, offering the townspeople of Thurman, Texas (pop. 3,347) the rare spectacle of a grown man crying.

Ordinarily, Thurman doesn't have much in the way of drama unless you get all emotional watching peanuts grow. The town proper has a few stores, twelve churches, two gas stations, a K-12 school and a six-bed clinic that pretends to be a hospital, staffed by a doctor who pretends he doesn't drink. I sometimes do a little private duty nursing there. We have a café too, but it shuts down after two p.m. A nice place all in all though maybe just a little boring if you're used to a big city.

One thing everyone in Thurman wishes for, me included, is more excitement. Of course, there's church. I go regularly, twice on Sunday plus choir practice. In the fall, we have six-man football but not much else in the way of entertainment. For the women there's also Bible Study on Wednesdays with refreshments after. Ordinarily I enjoy that, but sometimes I have to slip away early because the other ladies in the group gossip so much. Such an uncharitable thing for church-goers to do, if you ask me.

One of the favorite topics is about how, years ago, Dottie believed that Ray, son of the richest peanut farmer in the county, would marry her. When he didn't, the poor thing ended up an old maid. I can't bear it when they start whispering about that, since I'm Dottie, and it was me Ray jilted.

Not that I held anything against Ray. If I started to, I just thought of all he's gone through. His first wife, a little Vietnamese woman he brought home from Saigon, never had children. Then the poor thing got killed in a car wreck. Since she was halfway to Lubbock when the accident happened, some claimed she'd been leaving. I never encouraged such wicked talk and tried to comfort Ray the best I could. We were getting along real well, just like old times, when he went off to the Fat Stock Show and brought Angelique home.

Angelique was as tall as a model and almost as pretty. Taller than Ray by half a head when she wore heels, which was every time anyone ever saw her. She had one of those low, sexy voices and always dressed in high style. Her makeup was heavy enough to make the ladies at the Community Church blush, but then they considered eye shadow a transgression.

Glamorous as Ray's new wife was, I could hardly blame him for preferring her over me. One thing about her arrival that did annoy me was how the chatter got worse, but I just held my head up and pretended not to hear. And, unlike some I could mention, I went out of my way to be nice to Angelique right from the start.

When Ray volunteered, like he did every year, to drive the Homecoming Queen around the football field in his vintage Mustang convertible, I kept Angelique company in the stands. She wasn't much interested in the game, but at halftime when the teenage girls who made up the court trooped out, she paid close attention.

"Would you look at that? Every one of those girls is wearing a frock dowdy enough to make a fashion conscious person puke." As usual, Angelique herself was outfitted in the finest Ray's money could buy, straight from Neiman's.

"It's not nice to be mean," I said. "Most of those dresses are homemade. The rest are the best their families can afford."

"Just because an ensemble is inexpensive doesn't mean it has to be tasteless," she said, looking rather pointedly at my dress. "Before I met Ray, I made all my own clothes. Even back then I was known for my style."

She talked so loud everyone around us stared, including some of the girls' mothers. I tried to distract Angelique from saying more by waving over a boy selling snacks for the Booster Club. "How about some roasted peanuts?"

"You eat peanuts? Disgusting!"

I paid for a package and shooed the boy away. "You shouldn't say such things considering how Ray—"

"You think I have to like peanuts because I'm

married to a peanut farmer? That's like saying I should eat dirt because he grubs around in it all day. For your information, I'm allergic."

"To dirt?"

"To peanuts. Just a tiny bite closes my throat so tight I can't breathe. Not that I'd ever touch any of those nasty goobers, no matter what. You know what they do with the surplus, don't you? They feed them to the hogs. Maybe that explains why half those girls down there are fat as pigs."

Fortunately, the principal had just put the crown on the winner's head, so no one else heard because of the cheering. I felt so embarrassed for Ray. He couldn't have known what Angelique was like before he brought her home.

She was still talking. "Doesn't it strike you as unfair the way they get to have all the fun?" She pointed a long nail at the field then smoothed a stray blonde tendril. "Why should the truly attractive ladies be relegated to the audience?"

I tried to be understanding. After all, it had to be hard moving from the big city to Thurman. "Now, now. All us old girls have already had our time. It's the young ones' turn."

"Old girls? Speak for yourself!"

I straightened up on the bench and tried not to take offense, but couldn't help it. "I was speaking for myself. Twenty-five years ago it was me down there on that field. It was probably the happiest night of my life, but you don't see me trying to rob some young thing of the limelight."

"You were in the Homecoming Court?" She sounded skeptical.

"If you don't believe me, ask Ray. He was my escort."
With that, she slumped in her seat. "Oh, I
believe you all right. I'm just feeling jealous."

"If you've heard those old stories about me and
Ray—"

"Who cares about that? I envy you because I
always wanted to be a in a real pageant myself."

"Surely someone so attractive has won her share
of beauty competitions."

"I wish. I was never even a contestant, but don't
you dare feel sorry for me. It just one of nature's little
jokes."

Before I could ask what that meant, she sat up
straight and puffed out her substantial chest.

"But why mope when I can start my own
pageant? And it'll be for ladies over a certain age."

I patted her hand and laughed a little. "Now,
don't be silly, Angelique. Beauty pageants are only for
young girls. Even if they weren't, you can't just go and
start your own."

"And why not?"

"Because people would laugh at you. And they'd
talk behind your back." I shuddered at the thought of
making a spectacle of yourself on purpose.

"Let them talk. What do I care? I bet even here
in Podunk, Texas, I can find plenty of ladies who'd give
their eyeteeth to be queens, especially since I intend to
require crowns and sashes, the full royal regalia. If you
weren't so small-minded and provincial, I might let
you join too."

"Maybe in Podunk there's a bunch of women
who are eager to make fools of themselves, but here in
Thurman, we have higher standards."

"We'll just see about that."

With that she stood up and stalked down the stadium steps to where JoKay Edwards, the fattest woman in town, took up half a bench. I couldn't overhear what they said. At first, JoKay looked doubtful, then she started to nod. The next day I saw the two of them marching toward the home of Mavis Worth, the nearest thing Thurman had to a mansion. By late October, all three were calling themselves Peanut Queens.

During the annual peanut festival parade, they cruised Main Street in the back of Ray's convertible. JoKay, who weighed over three hundred pounds, wedged the other two into a corner of the backseat. When she waved to the crowd, her upper arm slapped Mavis in the face. Mavis herself, despite her ball gown and a blonde wig, showed every day of her eighty odd years. Even Angelique had on such garish makeup — including bat wing eyelashes — that she looked ridiculous.

As the Mustang drove slowly along, she made exaggerated bows this way and that, almost losing her crown. I told Lisa, who stood next to me gawking, that they made an outlandish spectacle, but it sounded like sour grapes even to me.

From behind the wheel, Ray grinned with pride. On the street, boys whistled and girls blew kisses. Obviously everyone except me was having a great time.

Right after the parade, I went over to the convertible. JoKay had already disappeared. Ray, like the perfect gentleman he always was, helped Mavis out. Angelique still sat in the back, looking pleased with herself.

"Why, Dottie, I'm surprised to see you here after you made such fun of my idea."

I leaned close and smiled. "I just stopped by to apologize for laughing. What ya'll are doing looks like such fun. Can I still be a Peanut Queen?"

"There's one tiny problem with you joining. Only three will fit in the backseat. Too bad!" She yelled loud enough for everyone on the street to hear.

I saw Lisa huddling with other members from our church. By next Wednesday, my ears would surely have burned off, but it was too late to worry about that.

Ray, bless his heart, said, "If there's not enough room, Dottie can sit up front with me."

Angelique looked annoyed. "Whoever heard of a beauty queen riding shotgun, Honey Pie?"

"I don't mind," I said.

"Would you excuse us long enough for a little girl talk, Sugar Baby? I'll meet you in the café in a few minutes."

Angelique batted her eyelashes so fast, I felt the breeze. Ray slunk away. When he disappeared around the corner, she turned on me. "I just bet you wouldn't mind being up front since that would put you right next to the man you been pining for all these years. Well, you can forget about that ever happening."

My jaw dropped. "Why, Angelique. Ray's the sweetest and most sensitive man in the county, but I would never—"

"Not that it would do you any good," she interrupted.

She was so rude it made me spiteful, which is not the way I usually am at all. "If the only reason you won't let me in the Peanut Queens is that you're worried about Ray spending time with me, you must be pretty insecure."

"Me, insecure? In your dreams. If you only knew how funny that is. Just to prove I'm not jealous, I'll swear right here and now that as soon as there's an opening, you'll get it. Then you can get real close to Ray again and see how much good it does you."

I should have just forgotten the whole thing, but I wanted glory and excitement too bad. And, yes, a part of me wanted to get closer to Ray, especially since his new wife was turning out to be such a bitch (excuse my French). He had to be regretting his choice.

In spite of everything I knew, I groveled. "How long do you think it will be before there might be an opening, Angelique?"

She walked off with her mouth stretched into the widest smile I've ever seen. "Only till one of us dies."

Right then I should have known that Angelique never intended to let me in, but I couldn't help thinking how morbid obesity means someone as fat as JoKay is likely to drop dead any time. I also knew someone Mavis's age was due for the rest home if not the grave. Maybe I did have a chance.

Sad to say, I was right, at least about Mavis. She had a stroke the very next month. Of course, the Worth family chose me to nurse her.

A lesser person might have been tempted to help things along, and I'll admit I thought of the foxglove growing in my mother's garden. Even fixed up a batch. A dose added to this medicine or that drink would take care of things in a final way, but I waited for Divine Providence to take its own course. Sure enough, before the new year, like it was ordained, Mavis had a second stroke. Or, as the minister said at her service, the dear lady went to claim her eternal crown in heaven.

Afterward, since Angelique had said it out loud for everyone to hear, I foolishly expected her to call and schedule my coronation. Instead, on New Year's Day, Ray's convertible rode down Main Street with Angelique, JoKay and now Pauline Peeples in the back seat. They blew horns and threw confetti. All the women were in their fancy getups, plus furs to ward off the chill. How I wanted to be up there with them. If only I could shame Angelique into being as good as her word.

When she left the car, I marched over. "Did I misunderstand? I thought you promised I'd be the next Peanut Queen."

"Really, Dottie. Were you serious about wanting to join? I didn't realize."

I gaped at her and couldn't think of an answer.

"Of course, I would have invited you, but when I thought about it," she put an arm around my shoulder and squeezed, "Well, the ensembles are quite expensive. I'd hate to embarrass you when I know you can't afford better than that flour sack you usually wear."

I managed to smile like Mama taught me to do, instead of showing my anger. "I could always sew my own dress, you know. I'm real good at sewing. I can even do bead work. Please."

"Too late now that Pauline's one of us, but next opening."

Already, she was moving away. I ignored the onlookers and my own upbringing to say, "There'll never be another opening and you know it. Pauline's healthy as a horse. And so, in spite of her weight, is

JoKay. I've checked their medical records. You better let me in or I'll tell everyone what a fibber you are."

"Why, Dottie. I'm surprised at you." She smiled, only not so wide this time. "Sorry if I didn't realize how much you wanted to be one of the Peanut Queens. That's impossible of course, but here's an idea. You can be my lady-in-waiting."

"Your what?"

"Real queens have a court to serve them, you know. Why shouldn't I? And you'd be prefect for the job. There'd be some chores to do, like preparing food and cleaning up, but you'd get close to the fun-the next best thing to being royalty. And, of course, next time there's an opening...."

Since I knew now there wasn't a chance in Hades Angelique would ever let me join, I just walked away. Usually I can put on a happy face and pretend things will work out for the best. Today all I could see was a miserable life stretching out as grim as the nowhere town I walked through, as bare as the flat fields all around.

I was doomed to never do anything more exciting than waiting on sick people, cleaning and wiping up after them. My so-called 'career,' practical nursing, was really no better than being a servant. At least other women in Thurman had families of their own to wait on. I only had an old house that smelled of rotting wood and cat boxes. I'd live out my remaining years without even the solace of a fake crown to cheer me up. My prospects were so depressing that I couldn't put my foot on my sagging front porch step. Then, all of a sudden, I had an inspiration; a way to reclaim everything I wanted.

I turned around and ran right back to where Angelique was holding court with a bunch of admirers. I pushed through the circle that surrounded her and swallowed the little bit of pride I had left. "I think I'll give that lady-in-waiting job a try after all."

Of course, she had to torment me by saying I was too late, that already half the women in town old enough to run for office were clamoring to join the Peanut Queens' Auxiliary. As soon as the rest heard, it would be the biggest organization around. She said they didn't need more members, but I begged and pleaded. I humiliated myself so thoroughly that at last, Angelique gave in.

At the next meeting, held in the school cafetorium, I made my move. Since it was to celebrate the harvest, I suggested that every member bring a dish to share that contained peanuts. We had peanut stew, Thai peanut noodles, chopped salad with peanuts and peanut bread as well as peanut brittle, peanut butter cake, peanut chiffon pie, and peanut butter fudge.

Angelique, as I knew she would, turned up her nose at every offering. "A girl has to watch her figure or no one else will," looking toward me when she said it.

I just smiled and produced the tray of shortbread I'd baked. "Made special for you, Your Majesty." I did a little curtsey to frost it.

After the way Angelique had treated me, you'd expect she'd be suspicious. Instead, she said, "Why, thank you, Dottie. You're a most thoughtful and considerate lady-in-waiting." Then she gobbled down a whole cookie, ground-up peanuts and all.

At first, I had doubts a few peanuts would do

enough harm. For a second, I almost wished they wouldn't. Then I thought of every meanness, everything she'd taken from me, starting with Ray, and bucked up.

After the first bite Angelique choked, then wheezed. Her hands flew to her throat. When she realized what had happened, she stared daggers at me, but it was too late, because she couldn't speak, much less accuse anyone. Her face started to swell, hiding her eyes behind balloons of skin. When she collapsed on the floor, panic filled the cafetorium.

"What should we do?"

"Something. Somebody. Anything."

"Dottie, you're a nurse. Help her."

"Calm down. Anyone know CPR?" I asked, staring at Pauline who'd been hopeless in CPR training.

"Me?"

"You go ahead. Give it a try."

"What about you?"

"My osteo's acting up." I clawed my fingers to prove it.

Pauline knelt beside the fallen woman, ineffectually pounded her chest a few times, then struggled to blow air into her mouth. Between gasps she looked up at me.

"You're doing fine," I said. "Keep on."

She continued trying with equally poor results. Under the makeup, Angelique's face turned first red, then blue. Pauline shrank away. "Nothing I do helps. Won't someone else take over?"

She stared at all the other ladies who were huddled in the corner, but no one volunteered.

To Pauline's credit, she did keep trying, for all

the good it did. After another few minutes, Angelique's eyes glazed over.

I knew it was too late, but someone thought to drag her into Mavis' big Cadillac and take her to the hospital. There Dr. Summers, sober for once, diagnosed allergic shock as the cause of death. Ray surprised everyone by insisting Angelique be transported to Wichita Falls for embalming. Our local funeral director was especially shocked, but everyone else understood. Even in death, Angelique deserved the best of everything, as far as Ray was concerned.

After the service, he turned to me for comfort, of course. I tried to keep myself from hoping his attention meant more than friendship, that I might yet marry and have a real life. Most likely, after Ray had all the sympathy he needed, and once his grieving was done, he'd take off to some big city and find a new wife. But you never could tell. Things might be different this time. Maybe deep in his heart he knew what Angelique had really been like and wouldn't make that same mistake again.

Anyway, he kept coming around. A few times we went for long drives, even all the way to the next county for supper. That was more than enough to start the ladies buzzing.

At our first social after Angelique's death, they were all clustered around the punch bowl, gabbing, when I came in. Lisa came over to me. "I see you and Ray are getting together some, but I wouldn't get my hopes up, if I were you."

Much as it cost me, I laughed like I didn't care. "Of course not. I'm expecting him to take off to Denver or Oklahoma City anytime. Probably come back a newlywed."

"I don't know about the wed part." Lisa leaned close. "At my regular appointment this morning, Dr. Summers—mind you, he was a little in his cups — confided he'd discovered something really shocking."

At that moment, I knew for certain that I'd been found out. "What was it?"

"He saw it in the hospital before Ray had Angelique taken to that fancy funeral home."

"What?"

"Umm. Well. A *thing*."

"A thing?"

Lisa looked everywhere but at me, then leaned closer. "It was a penis. Angelique had a penis."

My mouth dropped open.

"It's true. Angelique was a man. Of course, I knew there was always something not right about her. I mean him. I always said...."

I couldn't respond. My brain was reeling. How could any of this be so? And - what about Ray?

Lisa stopped talking for a moment and rubbed her chest as if to soothe it.

"Oh, it makes my heart hurt just to think about it, but I guess you're not all that surprised, close as you and Ray are."

Now she waited for me to say something. All I could manage was, "I never knew a thing about that, that, abomination, Lisa Miller! And if you start gossiping how I did-"

"Oh, I'd never," she said, but looked longingly at the ladies across the room. "Course, I'll have to tell all the other Peanut Queens. Won't they be shamed? Sure am glad I was never crowned. Angelique promised me the next opening, you know. Now there'll never be another one."

My heart sank. Everything I wanted was slipping away. I'd never be a beauty queen. And I'd never marry Ray. Not unless I had one of those nasty sex change operations.

For a second I considered it, but what would I have to change to? Then I realized I had worse problems. Once Lisa's big mouth started blabbing, the talk would never end. I had to stop her and there was only one way. You might say I was about to do her a favor-to keep her from the sin of gossip.

"You're sure no one else knows." I said.

"No, I wanted you to hear first, but I can scarcely contain myself." She scanned the room with eager eyes. "Such a scandal."

The foxglove I'd extracted while I was nursing Mavis was still in my medicine cabinet. If I gave it to Lisa, Dr. Summers would assume she died from her heart condition.

"I'm feeling a little upset by all this, Lisa. Would you mind walking me home? Once we're there, I'll make coffee and tell you everything I know about Ray and Angelique."

"I thought you said you didn't suspect anything!"

"Well, of course, I didn't, but thinking back, I naturally see things in a different light." I steered her toward the door. "I'm wondering if that first wife was a man too."

"You don't mean it." Lisa hung back. "We really should tell everyone we're going."

I nudged her forward. "Think too, how you'll have enough gossip for the rest of your life," I said, which, as it turned out, was literally true.

STORY THREE

LETTERS FROM IRAQ
by Kadi Easley

June 19th—Northern Iraq

Dear Bets,

Wish you were here. No, scratch that. I wish I was there. This is no place for you. The heat, the sand, no showers. Not to mention getting shot at. I'll sleep tonight and dream of being home with you, and if we're lucky, our dreams will mesh, and for a few hours we'll be together.

Man, do I sound homesick. I'm sorry. I am, but that's not what's really got me down. Dallas is dead, and I'm having a hard time with it. I found him this morning when we went out on patrol.

It bothers me, the way he died. I went over the scene while I was waiting for the medics. I don't think he was stabbed by an enemy soldier. The knife in his chest was American and there wasn't a fight. Dallas wouldn't have let someone sneak up on him like that. He was one of the best.

No one wants to hear my opinion. Over here, I'm not a big city cop, I'm just a soldier.

I'm sorry to unload all this on you, but, well, I just needed someone to talk to, Babe, and for me, it's always been you.

I love you, Betsy.

Sweet Dreams,

Andy

June 22nd—Chicago, Ill
Andy,

Oh, Baby. I'm so sorry about Dallas. Dammit, I hate being so far apart. There's nothing I can do except tell you I'm sorry. He was a nice guy. I'm glad I got to meet him before you shipped out.

Now I'll worry double for you. I felt better some how, knowing he was with you. I know that was probably silly, but you know how I am.

I wish there was something I could do to help. Are you certain he was murdered? You know how you go off on a tangent sometimes. And Dallas was your friend. Don't let your grief blind you to what's really there. You know I love you, but, Andy, please be careful not to step on any toes. You're not in Chicago. Stay safe, Sweetheart.

I love you,
Betsy

June 24th—Northern Iraq
Hi Darlin',

We had a service for Dallas today. I can't even begin to tell you what that was like. It's so hard. He was so full of — I don't know — energy, life. He felt like we were doing something great over here. I do, too, but it was different with Dallas. He made all the hardship seem okay.

Do you have all my old letters? I know I've talked about most of the guys in my unit at one time or another. I need more information. There's stuff going on over here that doesn't have anything to do with the war. I guess there always is. An Army camp is like a small city, lots of stuff going on under the surface. I

hope you understand what I need, Babe. I can't get any more specific.
Love you,
Andy

July 1st—Chicago, Ill
Andy,
Sorry to be so long getting back to you. Your last letter just arrived. I hope I understood what you wanted. I guess you were worried about censors. I'm trying to read your mind.
Billy Mac is from Tucson. He's married with four kids. His wife is fed up with the service, and he thinks he'll be divorced by the time he gets home. (Is this the kind of stuff you want?)
Morgan is a loner. Not close to anyone in the unit, but you said you'd trust him with your life.
Weasel, (you never told me his real name) is always getting out of doing the hard stuff. Always kissing up to the officers. Nobody likes him much, and you hate being sent out on patrol with him. He's from Little Rock and lives with his mama.
Hotshot is a cowboy. Les Green I think is his name. He's from Montana, and you told me he was going to get himself killed because he's always trying to be a hero. (Don't let him get you killed.)
Hollywood is the surfer you brought over before you shipped out. He's gorgeous. (Sorry, it's true.) Seemed like a pretty nice kid to me. You haven't said much about him since you got there.
Wenton is an officer. (Yours? I don't remember. After a while, the names run together. Sorry, I'm probably not helping much.) You said he's arrogant,

and most of the guys in the unit don't care for him much. But, you also said he was a good soldier.
　　I'm not sure I understand that. If the guys in his unit don't like him, how can he be a good soldier? Those are all I can find. I'll look through the rest of the letters after work tonight. Andy, I'm worried about you. Don't get so wrapped up about Dallas that you forget to watch your back.
　　What kind of stuff is going on over there? I can hardly sleep nights now, worrying about you.
　　Please come home safe,
　　Betsy

July 4th—Northern Iraq
　　Happy Fourth of July, Babe,
　　We're having the sandstorm to end all sandstorms here. It's starting to taper off, finally. Dammit, they're calling us out. I'll finish this later.

Continued July 6th
　　Hey Darlin', just got back. One of our patrol units got lost in the storm. We found them. Hollywood was dead. Billy Mac and I were together when we found the body. He was shot in the back of the head. The big dicks are saying it was a sniper. Betsy, that's bullshit. A sniper's not going to be out in a sandstorm. Hollywood and Dallas were running-mates. He and I have been hanging out a lot since Dallas died. He thinks, well thought, Dallas was murdered, too. And now he's dead. I think the Iraqis are the least of my worries over here. I need you to do another favor, Babe. The stuff you found was good.
　　Hollywood's patrol unit was Wenton, Weasel

and Morgan. Steven Wenton, from Madison, WI, Donny Ray Moore, Little Rock, AR, and Denzel Morgan, Denver, CO, I think. I'll try to find out more. Can you talk to Sgt. Linden down at the station house? I'm afraid, Betsy. Really afraid, and not of the enemy.
Gotta go,
Andy

July 10th—Chicago, Ill
Hi Andy,
Spent Fourth of July with your Mom and Dad out on the lake. It wasn't the same without you here. I'm so afraid. I wish you could get out of that unit. I talked to Sgt. Linden for you. He pulled some information. I think I know now what kind of thing is going on under the surface. My hands are trembling as I write this letter.
Andy, you have to be careful. These guys are serious. Talk to Morgan, and keep close to him and Billy Mac. Keep your eyes open, and, for God's sake, don't let anyone but those two know you think Hollywood and Dallas were murdered.
Stay safe,
Bets

July 20th—Chicago, Ill
Andy,
It's been so long since I've heard from you. I know you could be out on patrol or something. I know it's hot over there right now. I'm watching the news every night, praying not to hear your unit is involved. This is horrible, waiting, not knowing. It was bad enough that you were in a war zone; now with this

other. I want you home so bad it hurts.

Sgt. Linden came over today. I've gotten to the point I don't even want to talk to him. I have information that you need and no way to get it to you. This is the best I can do. The two W's are not on your side. They've got friends higher up, that's why there hasn't been a murder investigation. Is there an officer there you can trust? Andy, be careful. Just drop the investigation and come home safe.

I love you,
Betsy

July 31st—Chicago, Ill
Andy,

I can't stand this not knowing. It's been weeks. I hope you've gotten my letters. I pray every night that you are safe. I live in fear that I'm going to get a knock on the door telling me you're...I can't even say it. I want you home so bad. Drop this investigation, Andy. They will kill you. I need you here. Please remember you aren't in Chicago. Please, Andy, for me.

Betsy

August 9th—Northern Iraq
Hi Darlin',

I've been out of touch, and I know it's been hard on you. Hang on, and trust me. It's gonna be okay. I got your letters. Got one from Linden, too. This is all going to be over soon. Billy Mac is on his way home. He was wounded when our caravan was attacked. We were so careful, but they knew our route, they knew our plans. I sent my information out with him. Linden is going to meet him and get the information to

someone that can help. I just don't know who I can trust over here except for Morgan. He and I are together 24/7. It's the only way we can stay safe. I hope you've saved all my letters. Someone from Intelligence will probably contact you and take them. Make copies if you want to keep them. I'm sure they won't give them back. This is bigger than you can imagine. I wish I could tell you more. Just hang on and trust me.
I love you,
Andy

August 15th—Chicago, Ill
Andy,
I got your letter today. A day late. Some officer from Army Intelligence came in yesterday and took all your letters. They searched the whole apartment and wouldn't tell me anything.
Andy, what's going on? I'm so afraid.
Betsy

September 1st—Saudi Arabia
Hey Darlin',
It's almost over, I promise. Wenton and Weasel are gone along with General Batts and Colonel Stephens. They were selling information to the Iraqis. Dallas and Hollywood found out, but they took their information to the wrong officer. They died along with I don't know how many other young men. It makes me sick that the General could corrupt those good men. Wenton and Stephens were fine soldiers, but the General found a way to get to them.
There is some good news. We're off of the front

lines now and hope to head to Germany soon. Morgan and I are going to be stuck with the intelligence guys for a while, so I'll be out of touch.

Hang on just a little longer. Without your help, I couldn't have pulled this off.

Linden said Billy Mac is doing well, and his wife seems happy to see him again. There's one happy ending in the god-awful mess. The next one will be when I hold you in my arms.

I love you, Betsy, can't wait to get home to Chicago.

Andy

STORY FOUR

TEN THOUSAND ACRES
by Megan Powell

"Do you want to play Scrabble?"

"No thanks," Brian said.

"I'll play," Amy's brother Peter offered. "Even though I'm not the writer."

Brian had a feeling he'd better get used to that sort of ribbing. He felt distinctly out of place, surrounded by mathematicians and lawyers and kids.

Amy and Peter were still in college. Brian was in his mid-twenties, and his fiancée had just finished law school, but the generational dynamics of Kiloran still cast them as kids. Everyone seemed to understand that he and Julie had more in common with adults than thirteen-year-olds or college students, but the Steinberg family tradition dictated that one had to pay dues.

But if dues had to be paid, this was certainly the place to do it. The Adirondacks were beautiful, a pleasant change from a mid-summer heat wave a few hours south. Brian didn't really do nature, but he liked looking at it from inside the lodge. The lake sparkled, and from this distance he couldn't tell that the water was the color of root beer. That was, ecologically speaking, apparently a good thing, and he guessed that the leeches also had an important role to play. He could embarrass himself playing tennis, ping-pong, volleyball or pool. The cabins all had electricity and plumbing, even reliable hot water. And there was a staff to take care of little details like cooking, cleaning, and driving into town over several miles of dirt roads. Ten thousand acres of paradise was well beyond his family's means. Brian had known Julie's family had money, but he was only now beginning to realize what that meant. He wouldn't have loved her any less if she'd been dirt poor...but he could definitely get used to this.

"What are you writing?" Amy asked.

"Just notes," Brian said. "This is classic Adirondack architecture. I might do a freelance piece." He'd definitely write about Kiloran. Whether or not he'd sell it was another matter. Advertising copywriting paid the bills for the moment. The last couple years of a bachelor's degree in architecture had soured him on the field, but he was finally starting to remember why he'd wanted to study it in the first place (aside from his parents' dire warnings about the fate of English majors). He thought it was time to seriously consider combining writing and architecture.

"The Nature Conservancy tour's coming through on Wednesday," Amy said. "They'll stare at the red room and the ceiling and poke around for a while."

The barrel-vaulted ceiling was impressive, and Brian was a fan of the medieval-looking metal chandelier in the main room — which was admittedly less impressive than the chandelier in the dining room. "I've been thinking of the red room as the fish room."

Amy giggled. "The fish room. I like that. Did you see the trout I caught when I was ten? It's hanging under the tuna."

"Do you fish?" Peter asked.

"Not if I can help it."

One of the official adults looked up from his crossword puzzle and barked a laugh. Brian was almost certain that Jon was the son of one of Julie's grandfather's brothers. There were five other cousins of that generation staying at Kiloran, as well as Julie's grandmother and four younger cousins.

Amy pointed to the trophies hanging on the wall. Most were deer; Brian guessed others were elk. "We've got names for the heads," Amy continued. Apparently Scrabble was less interesting than the Steinberg clan's new member. Proto-member. "When I was a kid I used to tell Peter they'd get up and move at night. Nobody hunts any more. The animals are so tame, it wouldn't be fair. You don't hunt, do you?"

"No." Though it might be nice to take aim with the camera. He was a passable photographer, and the area was gorgeous. He might be able to sell something.

Julie had insisted this was vacation. The last vacation before she became an overworked associate; the last vacation they'd take before the wedding in the fall. She'd only allowed him to bring the laptop after he'd sworn that he wouldn't use it for actual work. That would be an easy promise to keep; he certainly didn't like his real job enough to take work home.

"You know, this would be a great place for a murder mystery game," he said. "It's very *Gosford Park*, with loons instead of pheasants." He glanced at the pile of boxes next to the pool table. Pictionary, Taboo, and a truly evil-looking Jackson Pollock puzzle. Brian wasn't much of a board game fan, but he'd always liked role-playing. Murder mysteries in a box tended to be more socially acceptable than Dungeons & Dragons.

But Amy and Peter were exchanging funny looks, as though they'd guessed that most of the dice Brian owned had more than the traditional six sides.

"Maybe next weekend, after Gammuth's gone," Jon said.

"There really was a murder up here," Amy said with a certain amount of relish. "It was back in the thirties. A crazy guy killed Gammuth's husband and threw him in the lake."

"She's really sensitive about it," Peter added. "If you even mention *Law & Order* in front of her, she bites your head off."

Julie's grandmother was a formidable woman who played the role of matriarch to the hilt. "That's awful," he said. "What happened?"

Jon cleared his throat, and Brian glanced out the window. Ruth Steinberg was coming up the walk, accompanied by Julie. Despite the differences in their ages, Brian could see the physical resemblance. By conventional standards, the Ruth Steinberg in old photographs might be counted more attractive than her granddaughter, but Julie smiled more.

Brian hadn't known his grandparents and felt generally uncomfortable around the elderly. Maybe Ruth Steinberg had been soured by life, scarred by her husband's murder and her son's death in a car accident a few years ago. But Julie had weathered losses of her own: her father's death and her mother's breast cancer. The fact that she wasn't embittered simply proved that Brian had found a remarkable woman.

His heart skipped a beat when she came in and smiled at him. Brian was happy that still happened, almost four years after he'd met Julie, and hoped it still happened in twenty years. In thirty, forty, fifty, sixty years....

He looked at Ruth Steinberg, who hadn't been given that many years.

"It's beautiful out there," Julie said. "Put that thing away, Brian."

Obediently, he shut down the laptop.

"Xu can't be a word," Peter said to Amy.

"It's a monetary unit," Julie said, while Amy waved the *Official Scrabble Player's Dictionary* in Peter's face. Brian was proud his fiancée knew that sort of thing.

"Why didn't you tell me about your grandfather?"

Julie shrugged and turned on the heat in their cabin. "I never knew him. Neither did Dad. He died when Gammuth was a few months pregnant. She never talked about him much, and I never wanted to ask."

"I guess I can understand that." Brian shoved the twin-sized beds together. Their cabin had two bedrooms. In past years, Julie had typically invited two or three girlfriends to Kiloran, but they were currently the only residents. Brian was pretty sure that Julie's family realized they were sleeping together, (and they were adults, engaged to be married, so it was hardly surprising or scandalous) but he was just as happy that the cabin assignments left their sleeping arrangements ambiguous.

And the cabin walls were thin; seeing Julie stripped to her underwear reminded him of that. If the other room had been occupied, Brian would have worried about the headboard hitting the wall.

"It always felt...I don't know," Julie shrugged.

"Sort of like a dirty little family secret."

So much for amorous thoughts. It was his own fault for bringing up a decades-old murder. "Why? Amy made it sound straightforward."

"My great-grandmother only ever tolerated Gammuth. Even as a kid, my dad picked up on that." Julie sat down on the bed, which was too soft for either of their tastes. "But Dad was the only grandchild, the continuation of the family line and all that."

Brian nodded sympathetically. His family had its own rivalries and frictions. "So your grandmother didn't get shoved out in the cold."

"Her family had money, too," Julie shrugged.

"Amy said it was some crazy guy?"

"Yeah. There was this hermit, Howard Foster, who lived out in the woods."

"A hermit?"

"A bona fide hermit," Julie nodded. "Apparently he wasn't the only one. I think there was some guy living on the Webb's land, too."

"Everybody who's anybody has a hermit, I guess."

"He carved the mantle in the dining room, years before.... But anyway, my grandparents were staying here alone. There was a fire in the thirties, some damage to the lodge, and they were clearing out the place and doing some redecorating. One night my grandfather just didn't come home."

"That must have been terrifying, stuck up here all alone and pregnant." Helpless, he almost said, but Brian couldn't picture Ruth Steinberg ever being helpless.

"Well, not all alone. I guess there was the cook, maybe a couple of maids. They searched the woods, because they thought maybe he'd gone off hiking.

Gotten lost, broken an ankle, something like that. It turned out he'd been dumped in the lake."

Yet another reason not to swim in it. "So why did he do it?"

Julie shrugged. "They never really got a straight answer. Apparently Howard Foster was questioned, but I guess they didn't have enough evidence to arrest him. Or maybe they arrested him but had to let him go. I can't remember. And it ended up being a moot point. He died in a fire in his cabin a couple of weeks after they found the body."

"That must have been tough on the family. Not to have any answers, any closure." Brian couldn't help thinking that it would make a great story. And, following that thought to the logical conclusion, it seemed that the Steinberg's might have had a reason to want Howard Foster's cabin to burn.

Julie frowned. "You're doing it."

"Doing what?"

"You're spinning out some plot. Deciding where to hide the body."

"You can't blame me." Brian curled up around Julie, and tried not to think about how easy it would be for someone to enter the cabin and kill them both. "There's already a body. But I'll behave myself."

"I'm glad to hear it."

They didn't make it to breakfast, and Brian made it through the morning without thinking about the deaths in the thirties. But at lunch, the dining room fireplace reminded him of the story.

MERRY IT IS IN THE GOOD GREEN WOOD, the mantle declared. Brian wondered if Howard Foster had been merry when he killed David Steinberg.

Julie kicked him under the table, and he looked away from the fireplace. The chandelier, large, and fashioned out of antlers, claimed his attention.

"It's from Europe," Julie said quickly. "One of my great-aunts bought it. She sent her husband a telegram: 'Have found chandelier for Kiloran. Stop. Should I buy it. Stop.' And he replied: 'Don't. Stop.' So she bought it."

Brian laughed. So did the nine cousins and matriarch, though they had surely heard (and related) the story hundreds of times. "Did she buy the wall sconces, too?"

He knew instantly that he'd said the wrong thing. Before Julie could finesse a reply, Ruth Steinberg spoke up.

"No, those were made later by Howard Foster."

"Oh."

"We invited him for lunch," she continued. "We commissioned those pieces. He sat at the table with the two of us. He seemed a strange man, but I never dreamed that he was capable of murder."

The silence was complete. Brian thought Ruth seemed rather satisfied with her ability to control the mood.

"He used antlers from old hunting trophies," the old woman continued. "Some of them were damaged in the fire, but it seemed a shame to discard everything. Even afterward, knowing what he did, I never could bring myself to destroy them. Or that." She nodded at the fireplace. "It is important to remember, don't you agree?"

Brian swatted a black fly. "Well, at least I made

it a day and a half without sticking my foot in my mouth."

"Don't worry about it."

"How can I not? Your grandmother's terrifying enough when I haven't mortally offended her."

Julie laughed. "You haven't mortally offended her." She popped a piece of gum into her mouth. With Brian's encouragement, her addiction had shifted from cigarettes to nicotine gum. "She's a very pragmatic woman."

"Pragmatic. That's one word for it."

"When I was a kid, I idolized her."

"What happened?"

"I stopped idolizing people." She shrugged. "But I still like the fact that she doesn't take crap from anyone. Nobody'd care if she was a man."

"I scare easily," Brian assured her, "regardless of gender. You know that."

Julie gave him a peck on the cheek.

"How did he die?"

"My grandfather?"

"Who else?"

"Well, Howard Foster died, too, and you've got a morbid mind."

"Which is apparently rubbing off. I'd been assuming smoke inhalation."

Julie shrugged. "Me, too, but I don't know that anybody's ever mentioned specifics. It's always been a gruesome footnote to a gruesome story."

"Of course, smoke inhalation's pretty boring," Brian mused. "Maybe he was already dead. Maybe the fire wasn't an accident."

"A torch-bearing mob, perhaps?" Julie suggested. "The wealthy camp owners killing the man who killed one of their own? Or maybe the other hermits killed him because they were worried he was giving hermits a bad name."

"I like that."

"Gammuth's really sensitive, and not just about her husband. So if you ever publish any mysteries, they're 'contemporary fiction' when you're around my family, okay?"

"'Contemporary fiction' it is," Brian promised. "So what was the cause of death?"

"He was stabbed," Julie said. "Plus some amount of time under water. I don't know how good forensic science was in the thirties."

"Me neither. Something to look into when writing not-so-contemporary, contemporary fiction, I guess. So what happened to the knife, or whatever?"

"I don't think it was ever found. Or at least, it was never identified. Maybe it's sitting at the bottom of the lake, or out in the woods somewhere." She shrugged again. "Keep in mind I'm telling you family lore. If you're interested in facts, you might be better off checking old police records."

"That's not nearly as much fun," Brian said. "They'd probably just confirm that an unbalanced guy killed somebody and dumped him in the lake."

"That's not horrific enough for you?"

"It's horrific, sure." Not to mention conducive to insomnia. "But not particularly interesting. 'He was crazy' isn't much of a motive."

"So, it's not sexy enough?"

"Right. What about money? A mistress? Homosexuality? Family secrets? No, it's a horrible waste for...." Brian groped for fictitious name "....Martin Bernstein to die just because there was some Thoreau-wannabe in the woods."

"So who did kill Martin Bernstein?"

"And what did they kill him with? Or maybe he wasn't dead when they dumped him in the lake...speaking of which, how was the body weighted down?"

"I don't know."

"An anchor, maybe."

"Or a stone in the belly, a la *Rob Roy*."

He was definitely marrying the right woman. "That's a good one. So somebody had to lug the body into a boat and dump it in the middle of the lake. How big was Martin Bernstein?"

"I don't know about your Martin Bernstein, but I gather my grandfather wasn't a lightweight."

"So maybe Howard Foster—"

"How about Charlie Edgar? Better give Howard a made-up name as well."

"Maybe Charlie Edgar had help."

"The Webb's' hermit?"

"A disgruntled chambermaid?"

"An under-appreciated cook?"

"A jealous wife?"

Julie's smile thinned. Okay, then, maybe not a jealous wife. He could understand that she felt protective of her grandmother's feelings. It was bad enough that he'd stuck his foot in his mouth earlier today. How much worse if Ruth Steinberg ever accidentally read some 'contemporary fiction' that cast her as a killer?

"Crooked business associate?"

Julie shrugged. "Anybody you want. Anywhere you want."

"Probably not in the house itself...since I assume they checked the house, after he went missing, and there'd have been blood if he was stabbed. Unless it was done in the kitchen, maybe, or on a tarp, something easy to clean up...." Brian mused. "I think the killer could've gotten away with just cleaning the knife, that far back. So maybe the murder weapon just came from the kitchen."

"It could still be there today."

Brian's stomach turned. Sometimes there were drawbacks to finding the right woman. "Or maybe the killer used something else. A poker. A pool cue. A golf club. An antler."

"I like that," Julie said. "Pick a non-traditional murder weapon and just hide it in plain sight. Very ballsy."

"And Charlie Edgar is the perfect patsy."

"Why kill him, then?" Julie asked. "Why not just let him take the fall and rot in prison?"

Brian shrugged. "Paranoia. Maybe he knew something. Maybe he was involved, and could have identified co-conspirators. Dead men tell no tales."

"Then the fire should happen right after the first murder, not the way it did in real life," Julie said. "Charlie Edgar might be unbalanced, but he'll surely cooperate with the police if given the opportunity."

"Which might be a big 'if,'" Brian said. "Considering that he's a much more comfortable suspect than anyone in Martin Bernstein's social set."

"Good point." Julie grinned. "Want to go for a swim? Maybe we'll turn up a human skull."

"Or a leech." Brian honestly couldn't decide which option was more disgusting. "You go ahead, I'll watch."

"And come to my rescue if I start to go under?" Amusing thought, considering that yesterday she'd successfully gone across the lake and back. "Yeah, sure. But you'll owe me big time for daring rescues." Julie grabbed her towel and went down to the dock. Somebody, probably Peter, had the Sunfish out, and seemed to be moving along at a good clip. Amy might still be fishing with any cousins willing to assist. She'd announced that intention at lunch, and promised everyone trout for tomorrow morning. Brian never had been able to reconcile seafood at breakfast.

The porch door creaked open, and Ruth Steinberg emerged from the fish room. Brian smiled uncertainly when she sat beside him; surely a mortally offended woman wouldn't do that.

"I couldn't help overhearing your conversation," she said.

Shit. Brian glanced at the fish room windows, clearly open for ventilation. Why hadn't he thought of that? Why hadn't Julie, who'd been coming here her whole life, thought of that?

"I'm sorry, I didn't know you were there—"

She waved a hand. "Think nothing of it. I do hope you'll refrain from writing some vulgar story about your imaginary Martin Bernstein and Charlie Edgar."

"Yes. Right. Of course. I wasn't really planning to do it, I just roll things around in my head." He was babbling. "Coping mechanism, I guess. Even though it's not anyone I know, so I don't really need to cope per se...."

She smiled. "But it will be your family soon enough." She turned and looked at Julie, swimming circles around the raft. "She's a lovely girl, isn't she?"

"Absolutely."

"You're aware of her trust fund?"

God. She already thought he was vulgar, and now suspected he was a gold-digger. "Yes."

"It's relatively small. But she'll inherit much more from me," Ruth Steinberg continued, "as my will currently stands."

There was something about the way she said "currently" that Brian didn't like.

"My husband was by no means perfect. Since his death, I have seen no reason to draw attention to his flaws, no reason to cause my son or grand-daughter pain. I hope you can respect that."

"Absolutely."

"Even if you couldn't, there's your own comfort to consider."

"I'm more concerned with Julie's," he said gallantly, and truthfully. "And I'm not marrying her for her money."

"All the same, you wouldn't want her to lose it."

Brian took a breath. "Mrs. Steinberg, if you have a problem with me, I can respect that. If you don't think I'm right for Julie, you're entitled to your opinion. I want to marry her, regardless of what you think. If you don't want that to happen, you need to talk to Julie. It's her inheritance you're talking about, not mine."

"My mother-in-law never approved of me," Ruth Steinberg said. "One of 'Martin Bernstein's' cousins is still unhappy about the fact that money went to me and my son."

You had to be a certain kind of asshole to begrudge a pregnant widow money from her husband.

A certain kind of asshole, or someone with reason to suspect something was amiss.

"Wills were contested. We tried to keep things quiet, but there was more than a little unpleasantness," she said. "I take the family name very seriously. It would be unfortunate, even at this late date, for there to be any hint of impropriety."

Impropriety. He was suddenly uneasy sitting next to her. She was just a little old lady — but sixty-odd years ago she'd just been a little pregnant lady.

"I want to prevent that. Ideally, I would like to avoid making threats and hurting my granddaughter. Do we understand each other?"

"Keep my secret and I'll make you rich?" Except he didn't know anything, not really, and certainly couldn't prove anything about sixty-year-old crimes. By now, any physical evidence was surely gone.

"I asked you a question."

"I know," he said, and realized that the physical evidence might not be gone. If she had hidden the murder weapon in plain sight; if it had been a poker, or a pool cue, or a golf club, or an antler....

The more he thought about it, the more Brian felt he had to be right.

Ruth Steinberg had no reason to threaten him — threaten Julie — unless she was guilty. Unless she believed that guilt might be proven, proven in the court of public opinion and possibly a court of law.

"I understand what you've said." He felt like a sell-out, even though he didn't owe anything to the real David Steinberg or Howard Foster.

"I'm just an old woman. There's very little you can do to me," she said. Lied. He could at least ruin her reputation, and that might count for a lot. "And after I am gone, only Julie will be hurt."

"I just wonder why you weren't more careful."

She looked at him for a moment. "I suppose I've been as careful as was necessary."

Surrounded by fools — or people who could be bought. The perfect crime didn't need to be brilliant or premeditated or anything close to perfectly executed. The perfect crime was the one you got away with. Brian wondered if she'd been waiting for someone to figure it out.

Probably not. Ruth Steinberg seemed altogether too practical.

With difficulty, she stood. "It's time I checked on the kitchen staff. I hope you enjoy the rest of the afternoon."

"I'm marrying Julie, not her family, not her money." Except he was: he didn't get to pick and choose, he had to accept all her baggage, just like she had to accept all of his. That was what marriage meant. For richer, for poorer, in sickness and in health, relatives friendly or homicidal....

Brian shivered in the summer sun. Yesterday he'd liked the idea of being rich. If this dirty little family secret was the price — this criminally enormous family secret — well, he could live with being a sell-out, he decided. If it was a simple transaction, silence (which didn't really hurt anyone) in exchange for the life of Riley. It was just a slightly more extreme version of what he did five days a week from nine to five.

But of course it wasn't a simple transaction. Like so many other things in his life, it all boiled down to Julie. Ruth Steinberg had read him right: he wouldn't risk hurting her. He wondered if she'd

attributed his motives to greed or love.
He almost hoped she thought it was greed. She'd
murdered her husband. He doubted such a woman
could understand the concept of love.

STORY FIVE

LOVE IS A FOUR LETTER WORD
by Pam McWilliams

Tony Rissoli lifted his head off the mattress, and the dorm room started spinning.

"Andrew, please. You gotta help me out here." Splayed on his bed, limbs dangling from boxers and a smelly t-shirt, he begged his roommate for the third time.

The chills had gone, but now he was flushed and nauseous. He sat up slowly, eyes fixed on Andrew, and the walls stopped moving.

His roommate, dressed in jeans and a sweater, was looking at him like he had two heads. "Tony, you had to stand in line and beg to get that fuckin' job—unpaid, for Christ's sake. There's gotta be a long list of suckers happy to fill in for you. Just call your boss."

It was their freshman year at Columbia University. Initially, Andrew had acted like a decent guy. But this semester his whole attitude was different. Four letter words, a sudden harsh New York accent. Tony wondered if he talked like that outside the dorm.

"I've only worked there four times, Andrew. I want them to think I'm reliable."

"For Christ's sake, you're sick. You look like death."

"I feel like...."

It was a virus that felt like the flu. Like death. And still he couldn't get Lena out of his stupid head. It was over. Six weeks of torture — like an addict trying to dry out. She'd called one last time ten days ago. He'd picked up the phone, heard her voice, and said nothing. But since then, her words, her heartbroken voice, were like a stuck recording that he couldn't turn off.

"It's more than just the virus," he told Andrew. "It's Lena."

"Christ, you're fuckin' lovesick? Jesus, man, you broke up with her."

"But do you think I did the right thing?"

Andrew considered the question.

"Worried you'll never meet anyone as beautiful?"

Tony hung his head. "God, no. It was so much more than that."

"Yeah, you did the right thing. Face it, you were obsessed with her. Not good in your situation."

"So, will you help me out? Andrew, I need a future. It would kill me to screw this up on top of everything." On top of Lena.

Andrew glanced at the framed posters lining the wall above Tony's bed. Several Ken Burns films, *The Civil War*, *Mark Twain*, *Brooklyn Bridge*; the Michael Moore film *Bowling for Columbine*, and recent releases, *My Architect* and *The Fog of War*. All documentaries, except for one poster which announced the debut of StoryCorps in Grand Central Terminal. COME SHARE YOUR STORY, it said, and beneath, a quote from Studs Terkel: "We know there's an architect, but who hung the iron? Who were the brick masons? StoryCorps is celebrating the lives of the uncelebrated."

"Two sessions, you said?" Andrew asked.

"Right. Each about forty minutes, usually less. And it's interesting."

"Okay, but this is gonna cost you. This is a major inconvenience."

"Okay, what?" Tony asked.

"One hundred bills. Fifty a pop."

"Like you need the money," Tony said, exasperated.

"I might. In the alternative, you can repay me with a favor."

"Legal?"

"I am not my father."

"Sure you don't want to be?"

Andrew laughed. "I'm offended, Tony. But if you don't like the favor I need, you can pay me the hundred bucks."

"Love you too, roommate."

"Don't give me that crap."

Tony watched Andrew walk over to the closet and change clothes. They did resemble one another, Tony decided, particularly from a distance. Italian, of course, with dark hair and smooth skin; similar builds, a little stocky but not heavy, just under six feet. It wasn't such a stretch for Andrew to pretend he was Tony.

"You sure you know what to do?" he asked Andrew.

"For Christ's sake, a trained ape could handle it."

"Remember, say you're me. The other facilitators on the schedule have never met me."

"Yeah, yeah," Andrew said.

"Andrew, please." Tony groaned, nauseous

again, clutching his stomach.

"I said okay, already."

Tony stood up and bolted for the bathroom.

Andrew sighed and reached for the wallet on his desk, glancing up at the watercolor, the lone piece of artwork on his side of the room. A beach in Sardinia. Shaking his head, he left the dorm.

Tony stumbled back into the room and threw himself on the bed. Drained, but feeling better, he drifted off...dreaming. Lena.

She had come to the party with some girlfriends. The place was packed, but bodies shifted and he noticed her across the room. Barely breathing, transfixed by her face, the other partiers jostled around him. She turned and saw him watching her, their eyes met, he kept staring — like some kind of geek — so he found himself walking towards her. Not like him, he'd studied his way through high school, little time for girls.

Lena laughed as he approached, but her eyes were kind. Exotic, something about her face, the dark hair which fell the length of her back. Medium-tall and slender, but with soft curves that made every nerve in his body jump. She spoke well, but with the voice of another country. Brazil, sensuous.

Talking, ogling, laughing, he was like a balloon, growing lighter with each passing second. Weightless, almost, as the drive and discipline of his high school years receded. He'd been at college for three weeks.

Lena (Rosalina) was eighteen when she moved to New York with her older brother. Their parents had died, he'd convinced her they would have more opportunities here.

Now twenty, a year older than Tony, she was working at a Wall Street brokerage firm, at first in the back office until she was spotted by a top salesman. He paid her well and had stopped hitting on her.

Before too long, much too long really, Tony made the subway trip to her Brooklyn apartment. She shared it with her brother, who was in the process of starting an import business. He'd gone back to Brazil for awhile to work out the details on that end. They were so lucky.

Lena took college courses two nights a week because she wanted to do something important. Maybe she'd be an immigration lawyer or a journalist or a teacher. After they'd been together many months, she confided, as they lay naked and entwined on her bed, that sometimes what she thought she wanted most was to raise a couple of nice kids, live to be very old, and dote on her grandchildren.

Tony, deep in his gut, wanted her babies to be his. This terrified him. He'd screwed up his first year at Columbia, he was barely passing one of his courses. He spent every free moment with Lena. When he wasn't with her, he was thinking about her. When they spoke on the phone, her voice drove him crazy. His life was falling apart. Sure he was in love with her, or maybe he was just in lust. How did he know? He wanted to be a great filmmaker, but he couldn't concentrate hard enough to be good, let alone great, at anything.

Just before Andrew reached the subway stop, the rain started. He cursed the April weather, but, acknowledged or not, the air held the scent of spring, its promise and myriad temptations.

He did sympathize with Tony, but Andrew understood the dangers of falling in love too young. His mother had repeatedly warned him, even though she still loved his father. She'd married at twenty, a man ten years older, charming, with an animal magnetism. It was just before the baby was born that she found out what he really did for a living. Stay, he begged her, the child is yours to raise as you want. She'd named him Andrew, a nice English name, the name of a prince. There were no Andrews in his family.

Andrew waited for the train, looked around at the other people. He wasn't exactly sure why he had chosen Columbia, but it was a good school, in New York. He was tired of running away from his roots.

His best friend at boarding school, the son of a German industrialist, told him, "Don't be so uptight about your father. Behind every great fortune is some kind of crime. You're an individual, but unless you accept your background, you will never be comfortable in your own skin."

His mother was fiercely opposed. "Get your degree in England or Europe, not here," she pleaded.

But for once his father took a stand.

"My love, he's a man now. Strong and smart." Andrew remembered his father's hand on his shoulder. "You shouldn't worry—he's never gonna work for me."

The train took Andrew into midtown, where he changed lines for Grand Central.

StoryCorps was a soundproof booth situated off the main concourse near the entrance to Track 14. Glowing like a spaceship, it beckoned to Andrew from across the terminal.

He had seen it once, just before Christmas. Tony had pointed it out when they had come downtown after exams to see a play and get drunk. Tony had not yet talked his way into a job there, but from the beginning, the aspiring documentary maker was enamored with the idea. StoryCorps was the brainchild of an award-winning radio producer, an oral history project designed to encourage people to share their life experiences with one another. The Grand Central location was the first of several planned throughout the country.

"Can you imagine all the extraordinary stories that ordinary people have locked away?"

Tony's enthusiasm was lost on Andrew. Who cared about ordinary people — did anyone want to be ordinary?

The little building was cheerful, brightly colored with rows of small human silhouettes dotting the translucent walls. LISTENING IS AN ACT OF LOVE the electric sign flashed at passersby, who were invited to press a button on the outside wall. Andrew jabbed at the button and heard a recording, a tiny fragment of someone's life story.

A man's voice asked, "And what happened next?"

"They start to drill holes in wall from other side." An old woman's voice, German perhaps, trembled as she spoke.

"People around us have hammers, and they pound at cracks. Strangers kiss each other, dance on wall. So much noise, it hurt my ears but I no care. My son, forty-five years old with bad back, he carry me through rubble. He stumble, but he no drop me. I close my eyes because of dust, but when I open them...." She was weeping.

Andrew nodded. Fall of the Berlin Wall, 1989. Maybe this would be entertaining.

He peered through a narrow window in the door before opening it. The facilitator looked like somebody's mother, a few lines on her face, some gray hairs. His own mother always surprised people. Still a stunning woman, she was only forty years old.

"Hello, are you Tony Rissoli?" she inquired with a smile.

"Yes," he said, easing into the lie.

She looked at her watch. "The next two people are due in ten minutes. Everything's ready. You know what to do?"

Andrew nodded.

"Good. I'll be going then."

Andrew looked at the schedule. Susan Tiller and Ben Crawford. He checked out the room, the recording equipment.

The door opened and a couple walked in, mid-conversation.

"Susan, I promised you lunch at a nice restaurant. What are we doing here?" Surprised, but pleasant about it. Thirty-ish, was Andrew's guess. The man looked comfortable in his nice suit.

Smiling, the girl said, "You said I could pick the place."

She had a nice voice, slightly husky around the edges. She opened her purse and paid the ten dollar fee. Slender, dressed in a simple gray dress, she wore her light brown hair clasped back from her face. Very little makeup.

"At least let me get that," her companion said, reaching for his billfold.

He was tall, good-looking.

"No, I insist. This was my idea."

"Good afternoon, I'm Tony Rissoli." Andrew shook both their hands. "Please have a seat. Would you like a CD of your interview?"

"Yes," she said.

Andrew switched on the two microphones.

"I'll nod when I'm ready for you to begin."

The young woman smiled pleasantly at the man across the table.

"Ben, we've worked together for two years now, isn't that right?"

She reminded Andrew of a girl in his history class. Okay, but not a real looker.

"Yes," said Ben.

"I wanted to ask how your parents met?"

He wasn't happy with the question.

"Susan, they divorced years ago. It was very messy and it's a sore subject. Why are you—?" Firm, but still polite.

She interrupted, smoothing things over in her nice voice. "Ben, I'm really sorry. I won't mention it again." She paused briefly. "There's a picture in your office taken at your college graduation. You're standing with your grandparents. They look like a special couple. Can you tell me anything about them?"

A big smile.

"My mother's parents, yes, they're fabulous. They're in their early eighties now and they live in Seattle, so I don't see them as much as I'd like."

He was happy telling this story.

"They met in England during World War II. My grandfather was a fighter pilot; his plane was shot down. He was in terrible shape — a bloody mess, and, God, I can hardly imagine this."

His voice cracked but a few seconds later he continued, "The crash blinded him; the doctors thought it might be permanent. He fell in love with his nurse, my grandmother, although he was afraid to tell her. Once his other wounds healed, his sight came back, and he asked her to marry him."

"What did he think, the first time he saw her?"

She asked the question slowly, as if she knew the answer was important, life-changing.

"Grandfather said to her, 'I'm looking into the eyes of the woman I want to spend the rest of my life with.'"

"That's a wonderful story," she said, smiling.

"Yes, well." Ben shrugged. "Are we done?"

"Not quite," she replied. "Ben, there's something I want to say to you. I've worked closely with you for a couple of years, and I feel I know you really well. You're an incredible person, but I've watched you mess up your personal life over and over. You have horrible taste in women."

Andrew, who had started to drift off, looked on with new interest. Was she nuts?

Ben's face was red, angry, "Susan, it's none of—"

"My business, I know. And you're right. But the reason I'm telling you this is because I've admired you for a long time. I know you're a good person, and I've developed a major crush on you, but it's more than that really."

Definitely crazy, Andrew decided, but at the

same time a little surprised she hadn't worn different clothes, done something more.

"Susan, do you know what you're saying, what you've done to our working relationship?"

Ben's voice was much too loud for the small space. He lowered his eyes. Andrew wondered whether he was embarrassed. Maybe women did this to him all the time, but probably not at StoryCorps.

"I know exactly what I've done. Which is why I've accepted another job and won't be coming back to the office with you."

"What?" Ben demanded, surprise overtaking his anger.

"Ben, I've put you in a very awkward situation. I can't continue as your assistant. You're between projects now; they'll replace me tomorrow."

The seconds ticked by. Andrew stole a look at his watch. Susan's expression remained calm, not that she was. Her breathing gave her away.

Ben's face was unreadable, but then his shoulders shuddered a little, at least Andrew thought they did, and suddenly his eyes looked different, softer. Wow.

Susan smiled at her boss, stood up, she was by the door.

"Goodbye Ben, take care."

She was gone.

Andrew stopped the recording and said, "Would you like to take the CD with you?" Like a waiter, asking about the leftover food.

Ben smiled, uncomfortable.

"Was that the craziest thing you ever heard? No, I don't want the CD. I'm really sorry about all this."

He left.

Andrew was surprised — that he was mistaken about Ben, that he felt sorry for Susan.

Two minutes later the door opened and Ben was back, looking sheepish.

"Excuse me, but I think I will take that CD."

He grinned as he left.

Andrew shook his head, smiling. Could people's lives change, unexpectedly, so quickly? Things might not work out between Ben and Susan, but even so. And suddenly his mind was back in history class, on the girl who sat beside him. Really smart, based on her comments. From time to time, she'd turn and ask him a question. Why? Did she like him? Just then the door opened again. Andrew was unprepared. Two men this time, one looked Hispanic.

Andrew said, "Oh, hello," and quickly checked the schedule. "You are Ricardo da Costa and Farzin Zahedi?"

He had no trouble with foreign names; he was fluent in several languages.

"That's us. You have a name?"

Definitely some kind of Latino, based on the accent. His thick, dark hair was pulled back into a short pony tail.

"Yes, forgive me. The name's Rissoli," Andrew said, extending his hand, noting the muscular arms, the tattoo.

He was turning toward the other man — much thinner, a plaid shirt and old khakis — when the Latino said, "Let me guess, your first name is Tony." The languid words rolled off his tongue, making them easy to understand in spite of the thick accent.

A small coincidence, really, the fact that Tony was his father's name as well as his roommate's. It was very common in Italian families. Andrew, however, was different than his father, better, smarter. Wasn't that the major lesson of his young life? And who was this little shit talking down to him? "Actually, it's Mister Rissoli," he answered in a polished tone, his vowels clear and consonants sharp.

"Oh, I see." A flash of teeth. "I guess we sit here?"

The men took their seats on either side of the small table, and Andrew adjusted their microphones.

Ricardo said, "Here you are," a crisp ten-dollar bill extended between two fingers.

Andrew accepted it silently, placing the money inside a locked drawer. The guy was a prick. At least he didn't smell.

Ricardo began the interview. "So, we are here because we are students at City College."

Andrew was surprised, he wouldn't have guessed. These men looked a little too old, but then City College was nothing like Columbia.

"Our professor, he told us about StoryCorps. He encouraged us to visit this place. He said it was an opportunity to learn something interesting about a classmate. He has given us a little incentive to come, of course."

He grinned at the other man, who smiled, his prominent nose dominating his narrow face.

"Farzin, here, is from Iran, isn't that right? I guess that makes you an I-Ranian."

"No, I consider myself Persian."

The man's first words were spoken distinctly,

but without an accent that might connect him to a particular place. He could have been born and raised in the United States, this man with the foreign name.

"So, tell me the difference."

"Persia is a kingdom with a glorious history. At one time our rule extended across continents - roads, bridges, the world's first long-range postal service. Persian artists and poets created works of exquisite beauty."

His face glowed as he spoke. Then he said, "My family has ties to the late, great Shah, Mohammad Reza Pahlavi."

Ricardo raised his eyebrows and glanced at Andrew, who was thinking, big deal, the Shah's been dead for twenty-five years.

"Wasn't the Shah thrown out of your country?"

"He and his family were forced into exile, yes, by the revolution."

"You say you have ties?"

"Yes. My father's family. My father and grandfather are dead, but the Empress Farah stays in touch with me and my mother."

"The Empress?"

"Yes. The last wife of the great Shah. Mother of the son who one day, with the help of Allah, will return to his destiny."

"You must be kidding?"

"No, I do not kid about serious matters."

"Well, Farzin, maybe you should tell me this story. How is the son going to take back his throne?"

"Allah is."

Ricardo interrupted him. "Please," he said,

shaking his head. "What is the real story?"

The other man paused for a few moments, considering.

"All right. When the Shah was overthrown and left Iran for what would be the last time, he went first to Morocco, but he was shortly in need of good medical care. He had cancer."

"This was when?"

"In 1979. That fall the Shah was allowed to enter the United States for treatment. He came to a hospital here in New York, where he met another Persian patient, an old acquaintance who had left Iran when Mossadegh was elected."

"Mozawho?" Ricardo asked, glancing at Andrew.

"He is not important," Farzin said dismissively. "Before the Shah left New York, he presented his Persian friend with a gift, a decorative metal box on which was painted a peacock, and on either side, the likeness of the Shah and his oldest son. A token present, but inside he placed jewels of considerable value."

Unlike Ricardo, Andrew knew about Mossadegh, who in 1951 became Iran's first democratically-elected prime minister. A power struggle ensued, and the Shah briefly fled the country. Mossadegh, however, had infuriated the British by nationalizing the Anglo-Iranian Oil Company. They wanted him out, eventually persuading the U.S. President to sponsor a coup. Mossadegh was arrested; the Shah returned to his throne for another quarter century, ruling his people with a new sense of determination.

Ricardo said, "You mentioned jewels?"

"Yes, the means to finance his return to power.

The jewels he left here were just one part of a small fortune. He traveled to other countries before his death."

"There is a box of the Shah's jewels somewhere in the United States?" A little excitement had crept into Ricardo's voice.

"Yes."

"Where?"

Farzin laughed. "I don't know. Would I be so stupid to share the story if I did?"

"Where is his son?"

"In Maryland, just outside of Washington."

"Oh," said Ricardo, nodding, "so he has them?"

Farzin shook his head, adamant. "No, the time is not right."

"You know what I think, Farzin? I think you are telling me a children's story, a fairy tale."

Farzin shrugged.

"We shall see. America is such a young country. People here don't understand the concept of time."

"You don't know anything more about these jewels?" Ricardo asked, disgusted.

"I know only that they are safe in the earth beneath a Persian tree."

Ricardo's laugh was tinged with bitterness.

"I think we are done here."

Andrew turned off the recording equipment.

Ricardo reached for his wallet and handed Farzin several bills.

"Why don't you buy us something to eat? I'll catch up with you in a moment."

Ricardo turned to Andrew. "I think he is either crazy or he just wishes to look important."

"Here's the CD," Andrew said, indifferent. Yet he was intrigued by the story. Ricardo accepted the disc, but shaking his head he said, "So, this is the crap that my professor thinks is important? Higher education, what a waste. Are you in school?"

"Yes, at Columbia."

Ricardo nodded.

"We are practically neighbors."

He moved another step towards Andrew—they were already uncomfortably close in the tight quarters—and pressed the CD back into his hands.

"There is no room on my bookshelf for fairy tales."

He was laughing as he left.

Definitely a story to remember, Andrew decided. Implausible perhaps, but was it really? The basic facts were true. President Carter had allowed the ailing Shah to come to the U.S. for medical treatment in 1979. This had so enraged Iran's new Islamic regime that a group of militants stormed the U.S. embassy in Tehran, taking hostages. The crisis would dog Carter through the end of his presidency. Andrew, however, asked himself only one question. Was it possible that an exiled Shah would hope to reclaim his throne?

Andrew was young; it was springtime. It was so easy to slip the CD into his jacket's breast pocket (Ricardo didn't want it), to delete the recording of the last interview, to cross off the two names on the schedule sheet, adding the words No Show alongside. He was forced to take the ten dollars, he didn't want to, but it was a loose end. Did the jewels exist? If so, where were they? A smart, well-educated person might be able to find out.

The next facilitator showed up a few minutes later, and after exchanging a few pleasantries, Andrew walked to the subway entrance.

The next morning Tony woke up disoriented, so much so that Lena was not his first thought. He smiled when he found Andrew's note, the bottle of Coke, and the saltines. Andrew wasn't such a bad guy, just confused. Dysfunctional families were a dime a dozen, but even so, Andrew deserved a prize for his.

Andrew returned from class looking unusually upbeat.   "The second appointment was a no show, but I waited there till the next facilitator showed up."

"Thanks, Andrew. I really appreciate it."

"It wasn't such a big deal. By the way, you don't owe me anything."

Tony smiled. This was good.

"What about the first interview?"

"Oh, it was crazy. Some love sick girl told her boss she'd been lusting after him for the past two years."

"Really?" Tony winced, thinking of Lena, but he breathed deeply, clearing his mind, moving forward one small step.

The car, a Christmas present from his father which he rarely used, was garaged on 115th Street, not far from campus. The sun was out, and Andrew was looking forward to the drive. He'd briefly considered cutting his afternoon class, but he enjoyed history.

She was already in her seat, chatting with another girl. He'd sat down, tapped her shoulder. Tell me your name, he'd said. She smiled. Pretty white teeth, a dash of pink lip gloss. Oh yeah, she definitely liked him.

Andrew drove his car west to the Henry Hudson Parkway, his destination a vacation house in Sag Harbor. The owner lived in a Manhattan apartment most of the time, but for two more weeks she'd be out in California visiting friends. This, according to her housekeeper, who had shared that helpful piece of information over the phone.

There was very little a person couldn't find out with access to a good library and a laptop computer. The old newspaper article was the key to everything, of course, but there were real estate records to check, maps to study, phone numbers to obtain, all of which he had done last night at Columbia.

Not that it was particularly important, but the Empress Farah had her own website, a way of staying in touch with her people. She seemed to divide her time between the United States and Europe. Andrew had even looked up the name Zahedi, identifying one man, dead for many years, with close ties to the Shah.

Andrew drove south, enjoying the view of the river. He'd always liked the water. He made his way across town, the Midtown Tunnel taking him to the Long Island Expressway. Soon he was passing an exit that would have taken him to Long Beach, where his parents lived.

There was traffic, not quite rush hour so he made good time, just over two hours. He parked in the quaint town and walked to the house.

The street wasn't far from the water. Quiet, no people outside. The house was a colonial, well-cared-for, its cedar shingles weathered a dark gray. White trim and shutters. Tall green hedges on either side of the house offered privacy from the neighbors. Andrew had never been to Sag Harbor, to the Hamptons, or to so many places here at home. Long Beach was relatively close, but it was a world apart. Vinyl siding was popular in his parents' neighborhood, their modest house so similar to all the others. Only their fence was different, taller. People could see through it, but it was there for a different reason. In the event of a threat, a switch sent an electric current surging through the metal wires. Once, when Andrew was five, the switch was turned on. Nothing happened that night, he didn't even know about it until the next morning when he went outside and saw the dead animals in the front yard. A few squirrels, a dead cat. The three ducks were fine, but they were lawn ornaments made out of concrete. The following year Andrew started school in Switzerland, returning home only for Christmas. He traveled with his mother during the summer, mostly in Europe.

The sound of a plane overhead drew his attention, and now he was walking behind the house to the pool, bordered by a tall, white wooden fence with decorative posts. There were no other houses, just the bay in the distance. The tree was in the back corner of the property, rising twenty feet above the fence, its blossoms forming a scarlet starburst. Andrew grabbed one of the fence posts, hoisted himself up, and dropped down on the other side.

The tree was similar to the one in the old photograph, but taller, of course. Flower beds edged with heavy stones bordered the fence. There was a bench under the tree, a slate patio around the pool. The back of the house was a wall of glass. Andrew heard a rustling sound; his pulse quickened. He looked around, seeing only the bird, fluttering on a branch, a blur of gray against the red. Should he be afraid? Physical fear—that rush of adrenalin—was okay, he decided. Fear of life was what sucked. When he jumped back over the fence, his heart racing with excitement, he looked around, daring someone to be there, but he saw no one.

On the drive back—today was only an exploratory visit—he stopped at a store, placing his two purchases in the trunk.

Andrew was thinking about his father as he drove along the parkway, the last of the daylight fading.

Their relationship had always been quite formal, like two distant relatives who rarely saw each other, uncomfortable in each other's presence. This past Christmas, however, Andrew spent three weeks alone with his father. His mother's sister was dying of cancer. Estranged for many years, she had asked to see her only sibling.

It was nice, dining together every night. Tony cooked or they went out to a restaurant. He was open to his son's suggestions, even though he preferred Italian food.

"But definitely no French," Tony told him. He was very mad at the French.

One night at a Chinese restaurant Tony was ebullient over the Noodles with Sesame Sauce.

"It must be the peanut taste. I always loved peanuts."

He asked the waiter for the recipe. The young man bowed, disappeared into the kitchen, but he returned and said, "Velly solly. Family secret."

Tony just smiled.

Two nights later they dined at home in the kitchen, Tony's favorite room. Frescoed walls, a smooth brick floor, it belonged in an Italian villa. They ate at the lovely old Tuscan table, which his mother had found years ago during their summer travels. Tony had prepared Chinese noodles as a first course.

"Whadayathink? I wanna try this on your mother."

When Andrew cleared the dishes that night, he found the recipe scrawled on the back of a Chinese menu.

During their evening meals together, Tony never discussed his business, although occasionally associates stopped by the house. Tony always introduced him.

"My son Andrew. He's at Columbia, the college."

"An honor," they said, with respect.

"Nice ta meet yous," they said sincerely, clasping both his hands between theirs.

Afterwards, Tony took the men back to his private study and closed the door.

At boarding school, the other boys had treated him differently, with curiosity or barely disguised contempt. All it took was one boy surfing the internet, and word got around. Andrew thought he might get kicked out, but he continued there until graduation. Then again, the brochure had promised a religious, spiritual environment, a school of learning that would take a little boy and mold him into a fine young man.

At Columbia he was much more anonymous; even if that were to change, New Yorkers seemed much more relaxed about that sort of thing—for Christ's sake, that TV show was a big hit.

The car was a surprise, but his father told him, "Your mother did real good with you. I'm proud of you, son."

Back in the dorm room after his first class in two days, Tony put down the phone. Life was looking up, even if his parents didn't think so.

The really good news was that he'd gotten the summer job with a local film company in Tribeca. Basically he'd be a gofer, but he'd get a paycheck along with the experience. There was also a good chance he'd be able to increase his hours at StoryCorps, something he was anxious to do because one of these days, the subject for his first documentary was going to come walking through that door.

When he'd first gotten the job, he and Lena celebrated by drinking too much beer, talking about how it might be fun to interview each other when they reached the point that they could keep their hands to themselves for forty consecutive minutes. Tony realized this was the first time he'd thought about Lena in several hours. Progress.

He forced himself to think about the summer class he'd be taking at NYU. Advanced Photography for Film Students. Columbia was a great school, but not necessarily the best place for what he wanted to do.

His parents had not been happy when he told them, late in his senior year, after accepting

Columbia's full scholarship offer, that he thought he might want to be a film maker.

"Not Hollywood movies, but documentaries."

"What?" they'd both said.

Their Tony—the wiz at speech and debate, plucked out of his Catholic school and offered a free ride at that fancy private high school only rich people could afford—he was gonna be a lawyer.

"How are the grades?" his father had asked him today on the phone.

"A little better."

"A little? You better hope they don't take that scholarship away."

Tony pictured the small house, the blue-collar neighborhood in Philadelphia. His father, out on disability with a bad back, was growing fat. His mom still worked at the nursing home. Twice a month she mailed him a care package, not just because she was an Italian mother. Her first son, Vincent, Jr., had died in childbirth, and after Tony, she'd miscarried twice. Life was hard, his parents argued, but Tony made them proud.

His desk, in recent weeks a disaster, was now neat and organized, and he was sitting there working when Andrew returned to the room.

"You're looking much better."

"Yeah, I think I'm over the hump," Tony said, telling him the news about his summer job.

Andrew mentioned that he'd been out for a drive, and was thinking about staying on at Columbia for the summer.

"I'm gonna check out some art history courses. I started thinking, I've been to every great museum in

Europe—that's gotta be good for something."

Andrew was acting different. Definitely an improvement, but Tony wondered what was up.

The Mustang was so sweet. Two years old, but in mint condition. The window was down, the radio was blasting a rock song, and now that he was past the road construction, the car was cruising. Andrew smiled at the poor bastards going the other way, headed towards the city. He glanced at his watch—in another five minutes, he'd be cutting the first of three classes.

Did he really think he'd find the jewels? Not necessarily. Even if they existed, it was still a long shot—in spite of all the facts he had put together.

But these were the facts. While the Shah was at Cornell Medical Center in Manhattan, receiving treatment for his non-Hodgkin's lymphoma, he was friendly with another patient, Arman Kashani, a well-to-do businessman who lived near Central Park. Real nice address, expensive. Medical records, of course, are confidential, and this information might never have come to light if not for the fact that Mr. Kashani had another home in Sag Harbor. One night he and his wife were dining at a local restaurant, talking about the Shah and the situation in Iran. Their waitress overheard part of their conversation. Her boyfriend was a struggling journalist looking for a big break and he contacted Mr. Kashani, interviewed him at his home, and sold the story to The New York Times. At this point, the hostage situation was five months old, and the world was watching and waiting.

The reporter had asked Mr. Kashani, "How much longer can this continue? Why were Iranians so angry that President Carter let the Shah into the country for medical treatment? Were they afraid that the U.S. government was plotting another coup?"

Mr. Kashani never mentioned the Shah's gift, the painted metal box, but why would he? The photograph was the key: Mr. Kashani, sitting on a bench beside the pool. The caption identified the tree as a Persian Ironwood. A few months later Mr. Kashani was killed in a commercial plane crash. His wife still owned the property, even though she was now an old woman. Was there a special reason why she was holding onto it?

Andrew parked his car in an inconspicuous spot in town. He was dressed casually for a walk on the beach, and he opened his trunk and removed the duffle bag. Even if he didn't find the jewels, what had he lost? A little time driving out here; half a dozen hours on the research. The important thing, he decided, was that he was doing something, taking a risk, finding out who he wanted to be. Regardless of what happened today, he was going to ask the girl, Hope, if she wanted to grab a cup of coffee.

He walked along the beach and approached the house from the back. He jumped the fence and removed the shovel and metal detector from his bag. He turned on the machine, moving it along the ground near the base of the tree. At the first hint of a beep, he quickly turned it off and picked up the shovel. His digging produced a large pile of rusty nails, probably dropped years ago by the builder.

Andrew was busy shoveling the dirt back into the hole, and didn't see the two men jump the fence. He looked up, startled, realizing with regret that he shouldn't be. It was Ricardo, with another Latino. At a loss for words, he stood facing the two men, his hands resting on the shovel.

"Well Tony, I see we meet again," Ricardo said, the sneer in his languid voice more pronounced.

"My name's not Tony," he said angrily, but not to correct the lie. What did it matter? He said it because all his life, he'd been told that he couldn't grow up to be his father. He was Andrew, a future....

"That's right. My mistake. But the important thing, *Mister* Rissoli, is that I don't like guys who hurt my little sister."

As Andrew's eyes widened in surprise, all the pieces fell into place. He opened his mouth and tried to find some words, while Ricardo, whose name was actually Luiz, picked up a large rock from the flower bed and hit Andrew on the back of the head. Barely conscious, he felt his body crumple and fall to the ground.

"Throw him in," Luiz instructed the other man.

Andrew fell to the bottom of the pool and gradually floated to the surface, face-down. He was dreaming, he must be - had they met for coffee yet? He was floating, letting the ocean's gentle waves carry him into shore. Hope was running along the beach, towards him. Her light brown hair was loose, blowing across her face. All he could see was her smile, pretty white teeth, and....

"Let us wait ten minutes," Luiz said, and the other man looked at his watch. Luiz was wearing gloves.

Luiz carried the large stone over to the flower bed and put it back in place. Some blood and a few strands of dark hair clung to the rock.

The two men chatted about business.

Luiz said, "I have a new customer in Long Beach."

"Good."

"Yes, it is very good. He wants to buy a large amount, a regular supply."

The other man looked at the pool, nodding at the body. "How did you know he would believe the story?"

"A guy like that who turns his back on the love of a beautiful woman, he wants one of two things. Fame or money."

The other man nodded. "Do you think your sister will get over him?"

"She is young; she will. The passion for a dead person, it does not last."

"He looks dead to me."

Luiz checked his watch.

"Yes. Time is up. We should go."

Author's Note: StoryCorps is a real place, but apart from the physical description, all the characters and conversations are fictitious. I apologize for using such a noble place as a setting for deception, but at the same time, it fired my imagination.

STORY SIX

DEATH IN THE GARDENS
by Roberta Rogow

They said the walls of Babylon could never be scaled, that the city was too well guarded to be taken. They said that only a madman or a genius could conquer it.

Darius the Mede would be the first to deny that he was a genius, but on the day we came into Babylon, I would have placed him with the Immortals, for his ruse was perfect, and we entered the city without spilling one drop of blood, neither Persian nor Babylonian. Those few who resisted the soldiers who crept into the city through the canals that led from the Euphrates were clubbed or made prisoner, by the orders of Darius, and his discipline was such that those orders were obeyed.

Yet, in those early moments of his victory, there was something in the general's eyes that looked like madness to me, his loyal scribe, who writes these words at the request of the Great King Cyrus. Darius was in the grip of some compulsion as he ran between those painted-brick walls and through the glittering bronze gates that led to the Palace of the Kings.

He went through the pillared halls unseeing, until we came to the famous terraces called Hanging Gardens, built with painstaking care by armies of slaves from mud bricks, filled with earth carried from far distant oases and sown with the seeds of plants taken from as far away as the lands of Punt, to the south of Egypt, and those mysterious regions beyond the eastern mountains. The gardens had been built for the woman who was the object of the Mede's obsession. His search ended in a little pavilion built at the very peak of the artificial mountain. It was not what one would have expected of a queen, barely a cottage, with two rooms, furnished with a bed, a dressing-table, and a small chair. There were two lamps that flickered in the night air, sending shadows across the painted walls, almost drowning out the growing odor of decay.

The queen lay upon her bed, her face half covered with smeared cosmetics, her sightless eyes fixed on the ceiling of her chamber, as if to find the answers to the questions that General Darius was asking in the clouds painted thereon. Her jewels lay scattered about her: brightly-colored stones set in gold brooches, rings and earrings, pendants and head-pieces. The floor was covered with the remains of her cosmetics, the powders and paints that were to disguise the sagging flesh and white hairs of old age. Nabotis, Queen of Babylon had passed her sixtieth year, and even after the death of the conqueror Nebuchadnezzar, she had held onto her power through his successors.

Now all her power was gone. She was only another dead woman, attended by another old woman who crouched in the corner of the room, wailing incoherently.

Darius turned to his men, the soldiers who had followed him through the canals of Babylon and into the city, even up the terraces and through the gardens to this little pavilion. "I thought I gave orders, there was to be no killing. I want a city to rule, not a charnel house!"

"Your orders were obeyed, Lord Darius." Cambeses, the leader of the guards, knelt in obedience. "Not one of the citizens of Babylon has been harmed."

"Then how do you explain this?" Darius gestured towards the dead woman.

Cambeses frowned. "This woman has been strangled," he pronounced. "It was not done by one of my men."

"Then who? Who took the life of Nabotis, Queen of Babylon? Now, when I had come for her, after so long...." If I did not know him better, I would have thought he was choking back tears.

A noise at the door of the pavilion drew his attention.

"You can't go in there!" We heard the voice of one of the soldiers, a rough voice with a mountain accent.

"The general will see me." That from another voice, a calmer one, speaking Persian, although with the intonation of the people of Babylon. The stranger strode into the pavilion with the confident tread of one who knew he would be welcomed.

"Who is this?" Darius asked.

One of the guards tried to force the stranger down to his knees, but the man shrugged him off as if he were a flea on a dog.

"I am called Daniel. I am considered a leader among my people, one who can speak on their behalf to the rulers of Babylon."

The man who spoke these words was one of the

most remarkable I have ever met in my lifetime of service to the lords of Persia. He was of the same height as Darius the Mede, and of the same years, yet he seemed both older and younger. His beard was not cut in the squared-off manner of the Babylonians nor in the pointed style of the Persians, but was allowed to grow untrimmed, in curls that covered his chest. His garments were simple, a linen under-tunic and a woolen robe ornamented only by a blue stripe down the front and twisted cords at the hem. He wore a small cap on his head, and carried no weapons that anyone could see, not even a small knife for eating. Nevertheless, there was something about him that made the guards drop their hands from his shoulders. He bowed his head towards the general, but did not prostrate himself as the Babylonians did, nor did he even kneel. He stood and faced General Darius as an equal. There is a word in my language, the language of the Hellenes: *Charisma.* Daniel had that power.

"Your people? Who are your people?" Darius looked the man over, judging him, as he had once judged me in the slave-market at Perseopolis.

Daniel said, "We have been called Hebrews or Judeans or Israelites. We were taken from the lands near the Western Sea, fifty years ago, by the conqueror Nebuchadnezzar."

The Persian guard fingered an amulet under his breastplate nervously. "This Daniel is known as one who can interpret dreams."

"The Eternal has given me this ability," Daniel said. He looked at the body on the bed. "General, I grieve with you at the loss of one who was once dear to you." He murmured a formula in Aramaic, a language

I had not heard since my youth in Assyria.

Darius frowned. "Why should I grieve at the death of the queen of Babylon? I have not been in Babylon, and I have never seen this queen."

Daniel smiled. "It was known in Babylon that when the Persian princess Nabotis came as a war-prize for the old king, Nebuchadnezzar, that she longed for her mountainous homeland. It was for her that he built these very gardens, and it was for her sake that so many Persians were captured and sent here to maintain them. She once told me of a young officer in the Persian army who had wished to marry her, but her fate took her here, to Babylon.

"You have spent a great deal of effort in preserving this city, whereas in other places at other times you have shown no mercy, putting the population to the sword if they resisted Persian advances. Why should you hold your hand now? It is logical to assume that you were that young officer, and that you have withheld your hand for her sake."

Darius regarded Daniel with narrowed eyes. "You know too much, old man. Why should the queen of Babylon confide in a soothsayer?"

Daniel's smile faded. "I am no soothsayer, Great King. I cannot tell what is in the future. I can only observe what is before me, and use the reason given by the Eternal to come to certain conclusions."

"In that case," Darius pointed to the body of Queen Nabotis, "what do you conclude from that?"

Daniel walked around the bed, taking great care not to step in the clutter of cosmetic powders that covered the floor. He sniffed at the body, then looked at the rest of the room.

"I see that she has been strangled with the cord of her own gown. If that is so, then the murderer must have been known to her, for no one else would have been able to get that close." He eyed the floor. "Moreover, the person must have been a Babylonian, for the Persians who came into the city wear the nailed sandals of soldiers. They would have left marks in the dust of these cosmetics.

"General Darius, if you would know who killed Queen Nabotis, then send to the market-place. Tell your men to look for a soldier in Belshazzar's guards. He will be trying to sell a set of earrings and bracelets, silver, set with green stones. Bring him here, and you will find your answers."

Darius nodded to Cambeses, who in turn sent the two guards out, to find the man described by Daniel. "You didn't say what you were doing here," the Mede reminded the soothsayer.

Daniel was silent for a moment, then said, "The Queen sent for me, because there was an event...." He stopped, then went on. "Last night, Belshazzar gave a feast."

"Why don't you call him by his title?" I asked. The two men turned to me in surprise. A scribe's duty is to record, not to interpose himself into the scene. I must confess that I wilted under the intensity of those two pairs of eyes, the dark black ones of the Mede and the lighter, almost green eyes of the man they now call Prophet.

Daniel said, "Although he was brutal and sinful, the conqueror Nebuchadnezzar deserved the title of king. He took many prisoners back to Babylon, my family among them, but his rule was just. He considered the people of this city as his children, and saw to their welfare. The Eternal punished him for his wickedness, but he repented and in the end acknowledged the might of the Eternal." Daniel's voice hardened as he continued.

"Belshazzar cared for nothing but his own pleasures, and those of his reckless companions. He had taken the sacred vessels from the Temple of Solomon, those that were part of the booty taken by Nebuchadnezzar, to be used at his feast. The conqueror had treated the vessels with respect, storing them in a place sacred to the gods of Babylon. Belshazzar took them and defiled them, putting them to unholy uses."

Daniel's lips were tight with disdain. "For this, and for other sins, he was given a sign. A hand came out of the mist and wrote words upon the walls of the feasting room, but no one could interpret them. It was the old queen who had Belshazzar send for me, to come and read the writing on the wall."

"And what did it say?" Darius asked, intrigued.

"The words were 'Mene, mene, tekel, upharsin'."

"'You have been measured, and are not worthy,'" I said, automatically. Again, I found myself the object of intense scrutiny. "I know the languages of the peoples of the west," I said, in my own defense. "These words are in the language called Hebrew, a tongue used by those who were once the tribesmen of Israel. Some of them still live in the lands of the Assyrians."

"And the writing was true," Daniel went on with his tale. "For at that very moment, you and your soldiers were entering the city through the canals, and Belshazzar and his boon companions ran away as soon as they heard you were in the city. The Eternal has sent you to redeem the lost ones. Like the Israelites of old, you came across the waters dry-shod."

"If this Eternal is your god, he's mistaken. It was no miracle, but good Persian gold that bribed the caretakers of the canals and tunnels from the Euphrates to open the locks and drain the canals. As for walking dry-shod, that's another lie, for the mud of those canals is still on my boots!" Darius pointed to his leather boots, more suited to riding than to walking.

Daniel smiled under his beard. "Then that is the final proof that your soldiers are blameless in this death, for if one of them had come here, there would have been mud on the floor. As you can see, there is none."

There was another interruption. A group of priests of the goddess had come to remove the body of the dead queen. The old woman in the corner gave another howl as the priests approached the bed.

"Shut up, old woman." Darius snapped at her.

Daniel approached her, stepping carefully over the mess on the floor. "Semiraminis, do you know me?" he asked gently.

The old woman peered up at Daniel. "You're the Hebrew. The soothsayer. The one who helped the conqueror in his madness. Yes, I know you."

"Were you here when the queen died?" Darius asked, harshly.

"She sent for the Hebrew," Semiraminis quavered. "When he told her the Persians were coming, she said she would meet them here, in her own place, the one built especially for her. She had me bring her jewels and her cosmetics, so that she would greet the Persians as befitted a queen."

"Did you see who killed her?" Darius took her by the shoulders and shook her. Daniel laid his hand on his arm. The general let go of the old woman, ready to turn his wrath on the Hebrew.

Semiraminis huddled back into her corner as the priests carried the body of the queen out of the room. They would anoint her and paint her and place her body to be viewed by the people before laying her into the ground, as was the custom in Babylon.

The procession distracted Darius. "Where is the feasting room? I want to see this writing on the wall." He strode out of the queen's pavilion, with the rest of his court and Daniel following behind him.

We went down the paths that had been laid through the Hanging Gardens. The overpowering scent of flowering shrubs mingled with the less pleasant aromas of decaying leaves that had not been swept since the profligate Belshazzar had taken the throne. Slaves followed the general and his guards, until we had quite a parade to lead into the chambers used by Belshazzar and his court.

There are those who say that mud bricks cannot compare to buildings of stone. The bricks of Babylon were cunningly laid into elaborate patterns, varying the dark and the light clay, and painted with strange animals, birds with gold and sliver wings, and portraits of kings of former days. Gold had been applied to the lintels of the doors, and the ceiling had been left open to the sky, so that the sun shone on the gold, making flashes of light as the desert sun lit first one brick and then another.

A painted eunuch led us into the great hall. The

feasting room was large, painted with blue winged
lions in the manner of the Babylonians, and furnished
with low tables where the remainders of Belshazzar's
feast still lay scattered: plates and goblets of gold and
silver, scraps of food being fought over by dogs and
rats, flies buzzing in the heat. The torches that once lit
the feast had sputtered out, leaving burned stumps,
still smoking. As I looked about the feasting-hall, my
eyes were drawn to the space above the painted lions.
A great black spot, like a terrible stain, marred the
colorful paintings. I trembled as I realized that this
must have been where the terrible words had been
written and then effaced by a power greater than any
of the gods of Hellas.

In one corner of the room were a group of men,
penned in by the Persian soldiers. These were
Belshazzar's drunken companions, young men in kilts
and embroidered baldrics, now suffering the aftermath
of their excesses. Daniel looked carefully at the
prisoners, then said, "I do not see the leader of the
king's guards, Amarduk here. Your men may know
him by a cut across the bridge of his nose. It is likely
that he is the man we are seeking."

Darius looked about and found one chair with
arms, probably the one used by Belshazzar when he
ordered his revels. He sprawled into it, taking
possession of it and the city, with one gesture. Then he
frowned at Daniel.

"You seem to know a great deal about what
went on in the pavilion, for one who claims that he was
not there."

Daniel shook his head. "I did not say that I was
not there at all. I was not there when murder was

done. I was sent for...."

He was interrupted as the guards hauled in a tough-looking old soldier, with a scar across his nose, wearing the leather-and-copper tunic of the elite guards that were supposed to be the greatest in Babylon. They forced him to his knees in front of Darius the Mede.

"This is Amarduk, the Captain of the guards," Daniel said quietly. "Did you find him as I said, in the marketplace?"

"Hah!" Darius uttered a mirthless laugh. "Babylon changes rulers, but the marketplace does business as usual."

"And why not?" Daniel said serenely. "It matters little to a merchant who collects the tolls, so long as the roads are kept safe. The roads to Persia are known to be the safest in the world."

The guard held out two silver bracelets and a pair of earrings. "He was trying to sell these."

Darius stifled an oath, and half-rose in his chair. I wondered whether he had given those cheap bracelets to a young girl forty years ago in Persia. Then he controlled himself. "What do you know about the death of the queen?" he demanded.

The old soldier quailed under the force of that penetrating gaze. "I don't know anything about the old queen," he mumbled.

"Speak respectfully before General Darius." Cambeses ordered.

"Lord Darius, I only know that she is dead," the old soldier blurted out.

"And why did you kill her?" Darius came off his throne and stalked towards the quaking soldier. "Did she catch you plundering her jewels? Did you kill her for a handful of trinkets?"

"He did not," Daniel said, placing himself between the kneeling soldier and the enraged general. "But he can tell us who did."

That stopped the general in his tracks. "How?"

"Let me question him." Daniel turned to the terrified soldier. "When the writing appeared on the wall, the queen had Belshazzar send for me, is that not so? You came to my house, in the Hebrew quarter, and brought me to the queen's chambers, and she told me what had happened at the feast. I knew what it meant, and I told the queen that very soon the Persians would be in the city."

"You knew we were coming?" Darius's eyes narrowed in suspicion again.

"That was not difficult to foretell. Your army does not move quickly, and its direction can be seen from a distance. As to how you were to breach the walls, that too was known. The water sellers have been doing extra business, warning their friends that the canals may not be available for a few days."

"So much for secrecy." The Mede smiled sardonically. "Go on, soldier. What did you do after you took this soothsayer to the queen?"

"I stayed near the doors to the queen's chambers, and I took the soothsayer back to the feast, but I was not allowed inside the feasting room," Amarduk said. "But I thought about what he said, and then I thought, if the Persians come in the night, the queen may be in danger, and it is my sworn duty to protect her. So I went back to the queen's chambers, only she was not there. One of the slaves told me she had taken the old woman, Semiraminis, and had gone to her pavilion in the gardens, to wait for someone. So I went there, and found her...dead."

"So you took her jewels and ran for the marketplace, to grab whatever you could." Darius thrust the man away from him in disgust. "Take this thief out and do to him as is commanded by the laws of the Medes and the Persians!"

"And that is?" Daniel asked.

"A thief is to have his right hand severed at the wrist," Darius stated.

"A just decision," Daniel said. "For in this manner he cannot steal again, but he is still alive, to pursue another calling, albeit with one hand. Before sentence is carried out, I must ask one more thing of this man." He turned to Amarduk. "When you went to the pavilion in the gardens, why did you move the body of the queen from her place at the dressing table?"

"Marduk protect me!" Amarduk gasped. "You do have the gift of magic sight! How did you know?"

Daniel pointed to the smears on the soldier's tunic. "When I saw you, I knew that you had removed the queen from her place at the table and laid her upon the bed. You went through her jewels for the ones that she did not wear often, small pieces that might not be recognized. She had silver bracelets that she had brought with her from Persia that she never wore. I recalled seeing them in her jewel case. If she were waiting for her Persian rescuer, she would have worn them, and they were not there.

"As for your actions, they were written in the dust of the cosmetics. Your footprints told the story. You moved the queen away from the table and laid her out properly on the bed, out of respect. For this, General Darius, I plead mercy for this man."

"Oh, you do?" Darius stroked his beard. "What would you have me do, turn this thief loose? The law is the law, and what is law for one must be law for all. He loses his hand, and there's an end to it. Take him off!"

Amarduk looked frantically from one man to the other. Daniel bowed his head to the king. "I agree that the law must be obeyed, and a thief must be punished, but it could be argued that this man is no thief, in that he stole from the dead, who cannot own anything. He is, however, an accurate witness, for by his testimony he has told us who killed Queen Nabotis."

Darius frowned. "What are you saying? There wasn't anyone with the queen."

"But there was," Daniel reminded him. "Another old woman. The concubine of the conqueror Nebuchadnezzar, Semiraminis. The two women, one beloved by the conqueror, one who loved him but never received his love."

"Semiraminis?" Darius murmured. Then he gave the order. "Bring the old woman to me." The guards went off on their errand. "What about this thief?"

"Mutilate him and you lose a good soldier," Daniel pointed out. "Keep him to train your own recruits, and your mercy will gain you a loyal follower."

Amarduk groveled on the floor. "I served the queen, Lord Darius. I will serve you just as well."

I saw a glint of humor in Darius's eyes. I recalled how he had saved me from the gelder's knife, and knew that like me, Amarduk would now follow the Mede unto death.

"Take him to the barracks, and see how he does with the Babylonian recruits," Darius ordered. The guards removing Amarduk gave way before the pair shoving the old slave woman, Semiraminis, ahead of them.

"You don't have to be so rough," the old woman croaked out. "I won't hurt you." She eyed Daniel with suspicion. "Why have you had me brought here, Hebrew?"

"Conquerors and generals forget that slaves have feelings," Daniel said softly. "But I recalled that when I first came to the court of Nebuchadnezzar, it was Semiraminis whose beauty was praised. The Persian princess was merely a political pawn."

"I was the royal concubine," Semiraminis said bitterly. "Nabotis was queen."

"And after Nebuchadnezzar died, his heirs were not inclined to respect the women of the old king's harem. Even Belshazzar, the son of a daughter of Semiraminis, consulted Nabotis." Daniel continued, almost baiting the old woman. "After all these years...why now?"

"I had the poison," Semiraminis said. "I could have done it at any time. But I didn't. It was more fun watching her shrivel up into an old crone, just like me. Nebuchadnezzar loved her, but I gave him sons and daughters. He built the Hanging Gardens for her, but he came to me for comfort. And then he died, and the two of us had to watch everything he had done be undone by fools and ingrates, even Belshazzar, that drunken wastrel, was of my blood, not hers."

"And you strangled your mistress?" Darius
grated out, unable to speak clearly.

"The Hebrew said that the Persians would come
within the day," Semiraminis went on. "And she, she
laughed with joy, and said that it had taken forty
years, but her lover was coming to rescue her from the
clutches of the conqueror. And she called to me to put
on her cosmetics, so that she would look young and
beautiful again for him. And I had to do it! All the time
she was prattling, silly woman, about how he had been
a nobody, and her father had sent her to Babylon, and
they had promised each other that they would come
together again, no matter how long it took. And she
said how she had never cared for Babylon and hated
Nebuchadnezzar — how brutal he was, how mad with
power — and I could bear it no longer. I was placing
the girdle to her gown, and I took it in my hands and
twisted it about her silly, silly neck."

There was silence in the feasting hall. The old
woman fell silent, then twisted in a spasm of pain and
lay very still.

Daniel knelt beside her. "She has taken the
poison she would have given to Nabotis." Daniel
turned to look at Darius. "As I said, the old slave
killed the woman who took everything from her, even
her revenge. Now she is dead, by her own hand.
Justice has been done."

"As is true of the laws of the Medes and the
Persians," Darius agreed. He turned to his men. "Take
this...this body, and do with it what is done with the
bodies of slaves. Then proclaim in the markets and
temples that the laws of the Medes and Persians are
now to be applied in Babylon. As for you," he looked at

Daniel, "when did you know that the slave woman had killed her mistress?"

"When I entered the pavilion, I knew that the murderer was not a Persian soldier," Daniel reminded him. "But I was not sure that the body had been moved. Once I learned that the queen had been killed at her dressing table, it was clear who the killer was. She would allow Amarduk to appear before her, but he could never have gotten close enough to remove her girdle."

Darius frowned. "I suppose you want some kind of reward for this."

Daniel said, "I only ask that I may be allowed to speak for my people, as the occasion arises."

"Then go back to your people and tell them that you may remain their speaker to this court." Darius waved his hand, the signal for dismissal.

Daniel bowed his head. "Know that I am always at the service of those who need me, Lord Darius."

The Mede looked at the Hebrew with suspicion. "And do you foresee that I need the advice of a foreign soothsayer?"

Daniel smiled and stroked his beard. "Oh, you will, Lord Darius. You will."

STORY SEVEN

THE BURRO
by Heather Hiestand

Maria finally realized the truth when she picked up her photographs at the One Hour Photo. The answer, in the form of undeveloped film, had been sitting at the bottom of her Coach handbag for four months. If she hadn't been digging through it, searching for a stray paper clip for her homework, she never would have found the small black canister.

She didn't want to relive even one moment of the vacation that had widowed her, but once she had closed the door of her immaculate late-model BMW, she forced herself to open the packet. When she saw the photograph, she closed her eyes, remembering. Now, St. Jude curse him, she knew how, and why, her husband had disappeared.

They had seen the 'Caballos En Renta' sign as they were driven back from Eden, where the movie *Predator* had been filmed, outside of Puerto Vallarta. A horseback ride had sounded fun to Maria at the time, even authentic. The trip, a gift from her uncle, had been about getting back to her ancestral Mexican roots. Instead, they'd ended up doing a movie set tour through the jungle.

She hadn't expected Ken's equal interest in the horseback ride. Normally he'd have said something like, "What are you going to do, Honey, steal the horse and gallop off downtown to join the fifth of febrero parade? You're American, for God's sake."

Maria thought that being different, being not-American, had been what attracted Ken to her in the first place. He loved brown girls. Something about the tonal quality of their skin brought him back to his youth, back to his Peace Corps days.

But now, returning to her native land, Maria realized she hadn't understood herself at all. Ken was right; she was American. Despite the colorful baskets she wove, the cool cotton clothes she wore, the silver bracelets that tinkled at her wrists, she didn't fit in down here. She was too tall, and wore the wrong kind of leather sandals. Worst of all, her Spanish sounded accented.

That night at the Sheraton, she decided she'd had enough. "I want to go home!" she burst out, after returning from an evening spent sipping drinks out of coconut shells alongside the pool. Ken, saying he wanted to take a walk by himself, had refused to cab to Insurgentes to watch a dubbed movie with her.

"What's wrong?" he asked, flipping on the TV.

"I thought I'd fit in, at least." She threw her bag down on the brightly patterned bedspread. "But what are we doing here? This is just a tourist version of the American lifestyle."

He rubbed at the skin on her bare shoulder. "Babe, it's not like the brown's coming off. You wouldn't want to go completely native, like I did in the Peace Corps. You wouldn't want to live like them."

"Like them? I thought I was one of them. I was born here!" She rubbed angrily at her twitching eye. "I don't fit in anywhere, do I?"

Ken's gaze fixed on her. It seemed as though his

eyes, already brown and beady, condensed into little nuggets. She detested him at that moment, detested his easy, Boy Scout self-assurance.

"You wouldn't want to live here." He unbuttoned his shirt and scratched at his sunburned stomach. "You like your conveniences. And anyway, you moved to the States when you were four years old."

She opened her mouth to protest, but he held up a hand. "You wear a costume and think it's going native. Let me tell you, that isn't what native means. You're an innocent."

Maria tuned out the rest of the speech, one she had heard many a time before. You'd have thought his two years in Central America made him a whole different order of human. Maybe she should leave him. She could start over, finish her master's degree, and get a job teaching Spanish, even if she didn't sound like a native.

"You still want to go horseback riding?" he asked suddenly.

"You really mean it?"

"Sure, anything for my little mouse." He grabbed her arms in a way that would cause bruises to develop later, like copper-gone-tarnished bracelets.

The next morning Ken went downstairs, whistling, and made arrangements. Upon returning, he announced they were booked on a four-hour ride into the Sierra Cuale Mountains.

Maria blinked at the idea of four hours in the eighty-degree heat and humidity, but she knew better than to protest. The ride was her treat. She was merely amazed he could plan it so quickly. They grabbed a camera and suntan lotion, then went down to the lobby.

A smiling matron who spoke limited English picked them up in a mini-van for transport to Rancho Sueno and drove them a couple of miles down the main drag. They turned onto a dirt road, dust billowing behind them as they approached a ravine. Maria clutched the top of the seat in front of her until they descended the hill.

At the base of the incline, a skinny, mustachioed man awaited them. He took Ken's receipt and waved them into a shady area under a palm-leaf covered lean-to. They watched as the man placed colorful blankets on the tired-looking horses' backs and saddled them.

"Are we going alone?" Maria asked.

Ken shrugged. "The van left. They must have gone to another hotel. You'd think they could have picked us all up at once, but I guess that would be too efficient."

Maria shushed him. Time seemed immaterial to the locals, in the way of hot countries. The man finished with the horses, then disappeared into the ranch house without so much as a glance at them.

Ken stamped his feet on the ground, creating a shower of dust. He grimaced at her, then started to follow the man.

"Where are you going?" Maria called after him apprehensively. She hoped he wouldn't annoy the man. It could make their trip a misery.

"I'm going to talk to him."

"He doesn't speak English. Ken?" He ignored her and walked purposefully toward the ranch house.

Ducking back under the lean-to, she pulled out the bottle of suntan lotion and reapplied it to her delicate arms, wishing she'd thought to bring a hat.

A short while later, the mini-van bumped and rattled its dusty way down the hill, and disgorged a young couple. Ken reappeared in time to greet the new arrivals with a jovial grin, a neat turnaround from his previous surly mood.

"Lee North, and my bride Carrie." The reedy, blond youth held hands with his equally blond wife, who rubbed her other hand gently over a slightly rounded belly. "You're going on the ride with us?"

"You bet," Ken said, slapping his palm into the other man's hand for a handshake.

"What do you do?" Maria asked politely, feeling sweat dew on her forehead.

"Oh, I'm in transportation and relocation services," Lee answered vaguely.

Maria opened her mouth to get more information, but just then their guide approached.

"I am Jose," he said in heavily accented English. "You are ready?" Jose gestured for Maria to mount her first horse.

Maria eyed the horse nervously. As she inelegantly hoisted her forty-year-old body over the saddle, she realized horses were larger than had expected.

The Norths mounted as Jose paused a moment beside Ken's horse. Ken spoke to the guide in a low voice. She knew he would suggest they be taken off the tourist route. He loved a challenge, but that young wife was pregnant. She hoped Jose refused Ken's request.

The party walked slowly, crunching small bits of gravel into the dirt as they headed for the trees. Maria recognized acacia and fig from her guidebook, but primarily the sides of the concrete and dirt road were covered by thicket, broken at regular intervals by Colima palms.

She shifted uneasily on the hard saddle, trying to accustom herself. The horses spread out, Lee's horse leading the foursome. Ken, sitting tall in his saddle, made a valiant attempt to move his horse out from the rear, but the horse hung its head and always ended up where it started. Maria tried hard to keep herself from giggling as Lee's horse would trot to get back into the lead. The youth couldn't quite keep his seat when that happened, and he listed to one side. She relaxed. It would be obvious to Jose that they were just tourists and shouldn't be taken anywhere dangerous.

After a mile, Ken made an elaborate show of not caring about his horse's less-than-macho behavior by removing the camera from his pack to photograph passing exhaust-spewing VW Beetles with tourists and old Ford trucks with locals. Then the group veered off to the right and started up a slight incline. They were in a residential area now.

"Can you believe people live like this?" Carrie asked, her blue eyes wide with shock.

Maria felt, rather than heard, Ken's snort of disgust. Of course he'd lived in worse conditions than this, and thrived. They rode past a partially completed gray brick wall. Two walls were already finished, and a small man staggered across the floor with another load of bricks. He put them down with a clatter and a sigh.

"I feel like taking out all my pesos and handing them to him," Carrie whispered.

Everywhere they looked were little square houses in clearings. Lines of clothes were stretched between trees, getting dry but dusty in the rising sun. To their left, children played in a puddle by a withered palm tree. Maria smiled and said, "Hola," but the boys didn't look at her.

Ken threw the boys a five-peso coin each, and watched as they ran off into the thicket. "Maria, you know better. No Mexican is going to look a woman in the eye."

"They were children," she protested.

"They were twelve if they were a day," he retorted.

"I don't think you should've given them money. They weren't beggars," Maria said.

"Beggars, no, but they don't have much. If we'd had children...." he paused.

"You don't have children?" Carrie asked.

"No," Maria answered, wishing she didn't sound so surly. Carrie took the hint and pushed her horse to a trot.

Maria had lost interest in the ride. She hated thinking about her childlessness, and her husband's desire to have a family. If only Ken hadn't refused to adopt. She wondered, not for the first time, why he stayed with her. Ahead, Jose had disappeared. When she reached that part of the trail, she discovered a deeply eroded track heading down.

"Move it, Maria." Ken called. She took a deep breath and gave her horse her head. She closed her eyes in terror as she heard the sliding sounds they made on the rock, then sent up a small prayer of gratitude when they reached the bottom.

At the bottom of the hill drifted a sluggish river, algae making it appear a light olive green. In the middle of their passage across, the horses stopped to drink. Women scrubbed and slapped clothes against rocks only a few feet away. They were young and kept their eyes downcast. Maria didn't say 'hola,' knowing Ken would make fun of her again.

As her horse began to move again, one of the women looked up. Maria's diaphragm contracted painfully. The woman could have been her younger sister. Long, straight dark hair framed a soft oval face, with dark eyes slanted slightly over a straight nose. Her best features were full and enticing lips, which curved into a smile at the sight of her. Maria remembered when her lips had been that fine, before age had started to mold wrinkles there.

She thought for a moment that the woman, a girl really, wanted to speak to them, but she lifted a basket and turned away. Her hips swayed under a short yellow-tan skirt with black dots as she climbed up the low bank to where a burro was tied to a tree next to a Ford truck.

The creature looked pitiful. It shook its white-muzzled head away from the cloud of flies tormenting it and blew air loudly through its nostrils. Maria had a sudden urge to fan its flies away. Poor animal, it looked too old to be a beast of burden. The young beauty untied it and mounted, kicking its flanks when it didn't want to leave the shade.

Ken turned his horse in a wide circle as he snapped pictures. The beautiful young woman even posed for one saucy shot. Very out of character, Maria thought, but lost interest when Jose appeared from the thicket on the opposite side of the river and made an impatient sweep of his arm. Maria took control of the reins and trotted her horse out of the water.

An hour later, exhausted into mere endurance, they arrived at what, surprisingly enough, was a small café in the jungle.

"Funny, isn't it?" Lee said, stretching out next to them at a picnic table after they ordered Tecate beer and a mineral water with lime for Carrie. "I've been on tours over the years with different companies, but they all have these little cafés too. You'd think the money from a few drinks wouldn't be enough to make it worthwhile, but...." he shrugged.

Maria wiped sweat off her forehead. "I'm grateful for the drinks, regardless. And the scenery." She turned to Ken. "Have you gotten any good shots today?" She said it sarcastically, annoyed by his familiarity with the beautiful girl.

Their drinks arrived, transported by an out-of-place, middle-aged, caucasian waiter, and Ken took a swig before shrugging noncommittally. Maria rubbed at her dusty nose and stood. "Maybe I'll take some pictures now," she said, reaching to the camera still hanging by its strap over Ken's shoulder. He tossed it to her without a word.

She turned away, rolling her eyes. Her big, macho husband was clearly distracted, probably exhausted. He'd be a bear tonight. And they all smelled of sweat and pollen. But nonetheless, the clear jungle air exhilarated, and Maria felt happy to be alive as she stepped closer to the edge of the cliff. When she opened the shutter she saw all thirty-six exposures had been used, so she reloaded the camera and dropped the finished roll of film into her purse, then framed careful shots of the lushly green pine-oak forest above them. She dreamed of seeing a jaguar, but she knew there wasn't much hope of that.

After she took her pictures, she sat down cross-legged in the dry grass and daydreamed. There had been no ovarian cysts, and she'd had a daughter, a younger but no less beautiful version of the washerwoman with the jaguar-patterned skirt.

She felt a hand on her shoulder.

"It's time to leave," Carrie said. Maria nodded and stood, brushing off the back of her jeans.

They took a different route going back. This area had much more activity. They passed clothesline after clothesline of brightly colored T-shirts and shorts. Even at the higher priced homes, those with courtyards, she could see clothes drying behind curlicue iron gates.

Ken forced his horse to keep up with hers on the wide dirt and concrete roads, and Maria watched him look intently at signs of poverty as they rode past. She wondered if he compared life here to the one they lived in their pleasant, well-maintained home in Orange County. But they'd never had block parties there, in the middle of weekdays, like they did here. She could hear cheerful trumpeting of mariachi music and saw a flash of people through the trees that hid what had to be a small public square. It couldn't be such a bad life.

"Did you have a good time?" Maria asked Ken as he toweled off from his shower, a couple of hours later.

Ken shrugged, his eyes vacant.

Maria smiled. "I decided I like being American."

Ken turned away, not speaking, and grabbed a beer from the mini-fridge.

"I only meant that it's obvious I don't really fit

in here." She lightly placed a hand on his arm. "I think this trip was good for me."

Ken moved just enough so that her hand fell away. She tried not to let the hurt show, as he grabbed the hotel-provided book on the region and went out to their balcony. Maria decided to take his surliness as a challenge rather than a defeat and went downstairs. She remembered the hotel had a masseuse on staff in the gym. Maybe that would help Ken relax.

After making the appointment for ten that evening, she went back up. She stood in the doorway to the balcony, enjoying the breeze ruffling her crisp linen shirt. Even if she did need to give up some sense of her Mexican identity, she still liked the wardrobe.

She told Ken she was ready to eat, then went into the bathroom and dabbed a little perfume between her breasts and on the backs of her knees, hoping that Ken would be relaxed and amorous when he returned from the massage. However, Ken continued to ignore her at the restaurant. He merely grunted when she told him of the arranged massage, but at least he'd agreed to go.

As they finished their meal, their waiter came up with a shot glass and a bottle of cheap tequila. Ken's eyes lit up.

"Ken, we should go. Your massage," Maria coaxed, not wanting to deal with his drunkenness again.

"That was your idea, not mine. It's rude to say 'no.'"

The waiter grinned and poured. Ken laughed, and when the waiter didn't fill the shot glass to the top he said, "You can do better." The waiter topped it and Ken tossed it back.

After Ken's next shot the waiter offered one to Maria. When she shook her head, Ken drank that one too. Unstoppable, the waiter poured once again.

"Don't you think that's enough? We already shared most of a bottle of wine," Maria said in a low voice.

"It's a party! Manager's birthday!" the waiter said. Another waiter poured shots for the table next to them, and a third walked toward another table with a bottle in hand. Ken tossed back the fourth shot, then went a little pale. The waiter gave him a concerned look. "Let me help you to the door," he said delicately. Ken stood and followed the man out of the dining room. Maria found it strange; he usually had a higher tolerance. She was worried for a moment that the waiter planned to rob him, but no, this was an upscale restaurant.

"What a life," Ken grinned, not quite swaying as he returned to their table. "Why did I ever return to civilization?"

By the time they reached their taxi, Ken reeked of tequila. Maria swallowed hard. Her stomach hurt. She opened the taxi door, and Ken poured himself in.

"I like our life the way it is," she said hopefully, touching his hand as she sat down.

Ken pulled away from her. "Our life is shit," he said drunkenly. "This is for real, don't you realize that? Nah," he shook his head, "you wouldn't, pampered American bitch. This is a man's life. Men are men and women, well, women look like you used to look."

Maria's eyes were so misted with tears by the time the taxi shrieked to a halt that she bumped into an old Ford truck parked under the archway at the entrance of the hotel, its yellow paint nearly obscured by dust. My God, she thought irritably, don't these people have any pride? She left Ken in the hotel lobby for his massage and rushed upstairs.

"So long," Ken waved at her, weaving down the tiled walkway.

When Maria reached the elevator, she saw that her skirt was covered with dust from the truck. The dirt was impossible to brush off. She took a long shower in the marble-tiled stall, then settled down to wait for Ken's return. But exhaustion and the struggle to rein in her temper caught up with her. She fell asleep.

Maria turned over and slitted her gritty eyes, awakened by a grinding noise—someone must be cleaning the pool. Reaching out an arm, she tried to steal a bit of Ken's furnace-like warmth. She'd left the patio door open, and their room felt chilly.

Her arm didn't contact with flesh. Opening her eyes a bit more, she realized Ken wasn't there. In fact, had he come in at all? Usually she woke when he got into bed, and she didn't remember waking during the night.

She rose, yawning, and shut the patio door. The noise diminished, but not her confusion. Ken had had quite a bit to drink. Had he passed out somewhere?

Still a little angry from the night before, she dressed slowly then went down to speak to a desk clerk. He insisted in broken English that missing husbands were always golfing. His words didn't help, because Ken didn't golf.

After arguing with him for five minutes, she roamed around the hotel, looking for Ken with no success. At least he wasn't face-down in the pool. The clerk had promised to send the concierge to her when he was available, so she sat down to breakfast, trying not to visualize the newspaper headlines. Wife dines while husband lies dead in pit! Wife relaxes while husband floats face-down in ditch!

She shook her head. After the previous night, she didn't know what to expect. Usually, after an argument, Ken would throw his tent in the back of his truck and go camping for a few days. But he wouldn't know where to go, not in a foreign country.

She'd lived through it all, the tedious process of becoming a widow-in-waiting. Sorting through his belongings, interrogating the hotel manager, speaking to the police, talking to the American embassy. Notifying the airline, who sent down an assistant to help her through the red tape. One group sent a ransom message, but never made contact after that. The police assured her it was a prank, after they investigated. No one else ever made any kind of contact, but the police swore it had to have been a kidnapping gone wrong, and the vanished American must be dead by now.

Criminals, guerrillas, even the police had been involved in kidnapping scams in recent years, the embassy representative told her. Ken was a wealthy man.

The police insinuated that she and Ken had been too flashy, too obvious, too American to resist. They had brought this tragedy on themselves, by daring to visit what was really a dangerous country.

But now she knew the truth. None of those explanations were true.

Maria glanced away from the photographs and

picked up her homework. She placed it on top of the photograph, a picture of a sad old burro with a white muzzle next to a dusty yellow Ford truck.

Ken had gone native.

STORY EIGHT

DEADLY DESSOUS (DEADLY LINGERIE)
by Gesine Schulz
(Translated by Gunhild Muschenheim)

Karo picked up the telephone. "Karola Rutkowsky
Detective Agency. Can I help you?"

"Hello, Karo, are you alone?"

Again this hoarse voice, whispering. Karo had hoped to finally be rid of the creep last week when she gave him, after his fifth call in three days, the numbers of a couple of telephone dominatrixes who would be happy to talk to him.

"Listen, buster, this is getting boring. I—"

"But, Karo, it's me." still in a whisper. There was an undertone of 'you idiot,' but it wasn't said.

"Moni? Why in the world are you whispering?"

"Are you alone?"

"Yes, but can't you talk a little louder?"

"Karo, I have got a job for you," Moni whispered. "But you must come right away. Right away, okay?"

"I'll come, no problem." Not necessary to ask one's best friend what kind of job she was talking about. Moni knew that Karo in her other career as a sought-after and highly paid cleaning lady was fully booked and even had a waiting list. Thus it could only be a job for Karo Rutkowsky, Private Detective, whose jobs had lately, once again, been few and far between.

"What is it about?"

"A body," Moni whispered. "I don't know where to put it."

"Where to put it?"

"Yes. Right now he is lying behind the desk in the music library, but he can't stay there. It seemed like a good place during the opening of the exhibition just now. In any case I couldn't think of anywhere else in a hurry. All the VIPs have left. They are on their way to the Haus der Technik to listen to the lecture by Germaine Greer. By the way, do you think it is provocation or personal conviction when she calls on women to go without underwear? Well, I am sure our Alice Schwarzer will have something to tell her in the discussion afterwards. Now all the staff members have gone to their offices. But in an hour the library is opening for the public, and by that time the body will have to be somewhere else."

"But why?"

Karo had realized that she was not asked to solve a murder, but only to move a dead body. And that Moni would be her client. Moni, who as a qualified librarian working part-time on a short-term contract, was earning too little for Karo to charge her a steep fee. "Can't you leave the body where it is?"

"No. Absolutely not. The exhibition catalogs are stored here. I came by a few times during the opening to get more copies. I would be asked why I have not reported a dead body."

"Good question. Why haven't you?"

"Well, in that case I could have left him lying where he was and saved myself all this trouble. Do you have any idea how heavy a dead body is? And the guy isn't even particularly big."

"You dragged him through the library? Moni, *are you crazy?*"

"Don't yell," Moni whispered. "I was under stress. You know how much trouble I took with the display cases. And they really look good. Wait till you see them. I arranged everything in chronological order. It wasn't all that easy to make an attractive display, putting together the exhibit pieces with the photographs and the books. And in the last minute a fabulous new coffee table book arrived through international interlibrary loan—it's about the role played by lingerie in pop music. I put it at an angle behind Madonna's glittery bra, the one—"

"Moni, could we possibly talk about the body?"

"Then don't interrupt me all the time, okay? Now then, when it was announced this morning that not only the minister of culture but also the state prime minister of North Rhine-Westfalia would come to the opening of our exhibition, everyone in the director's office got so nervous that we all got the jitters too."

She paused and took a deep breath.

"So, I went downstairs one more time to make sure everything was all right. Well, and there he was lying on the floor, next to the first display case, you couldn't possibly miss him if you were coming down the stairway. The door of the display case was open, the book knocked over, the media were practically at the front door, the lord mayor was about to arrive any minute, not to mention all the politicians and other VIPs. With my contract coming up for renewal soon I wanted to make a good impression, and that would have been impossible if all of these people were greeted by a dead body."

"Moni, Moni. Nobody would have blamed you for—"

"That's what you think. Suddenly I wasn't sure myself anymore whether I had properly locked the display case and therefore could be accused of aiding and abetting. So I just took Madonna's bra off him, put it back in the case, locked the case and got a large garbage bag from the store room."

"Wait a minute. He was wearing *Madonna's* bra?"

"Don't yell at me." Moni said. She lowered her voice and continued, "Around his neck. He was strangled with it. I managed to roll him onto the garbage bag and then dragged him down the wheelchair ramp all the way to the music library, behind the information desk. You'll understand that he cannot stay there."

Several times Karo started to say something. She picked up the Leitz hole puncher, dating—like everything in her shabby office—from the fifties, put the cool underside to her forehead and sighed. Had anyone other than Moni come to her with this kind of request she would have turned it down without a moment's hesitation.

"Of course, I will pay your daily rate, Karo."

"Oh, Moni, as if—"

"And you will get the last two bottles of my great-aunt's elderberry champagne."

"Okay, okay, I'm on my way." She had to come through for her friend. And the elderberry champagne from Great-aunt Melissa was out of this world. Crisp and fruity, a summer night's dream. Moni was hoping to inherit the old family recipe one of these days. Karo was hoping with her.

"Come to the side entrance. I'll meet you there in five minutes."

On every advertising column, in almost every shop window, lilac-coloured posters called attention to the program of the Essen Lingerie Festival. The city fathers had recovered from their shock. They had called to their minds that they were broadminded people and as open to the Zeitgeist's moods as their colleagues in nearby Dusseldorf or even Berlin. Was not Essen the heart of the Ruhr District, and this, a metropolitan area of over five million people, countless theatres and more museums than New York? Even the mayor was now unabashedly tossing around words like garter belts, bloomers, corsets, push-up bras and g-strings. Unthinkable only a few months ago.

Then the city had enthusiastically accepted the bequest of a prominent Essen businessman: his villa in a leafy Essen suburb as a guesthouse for the city and university as well as a collection of cultural and historical interest that was to be made available to the public.

Great embarrassment swept through the town hall offices when it turned out that the distinguished old gentleman had collected ladies' undergarments. Some items were no doubt of historical interest, but the collector's zeal had not shied away from the present. Only recently he had bought at Sotheby's a glittery bra Madonna had worn on stage. Other items tended to be more practical than famous. The city found itself in the possession of a great deal of underwear and felt duped.

It being the summer slump, journalists across Germany jumped at the opportunity to poke fun at the dilemma faced by the Essen city officials. In the last minute, the people of Essen Marketing saved the day. The Essen Lingerie Festival was born. Exhibits in the German Poster Museum, in the Ruhrland Museum and in the public library were organized. Ki:motion New Media Design, in the course of an inspired weekend created a website that immediately was recommended for an international prize. The Missfits, a popular female comedy duo from neighboring Oberhausen, was rehearsing "Victoria's Secret." The program was to premier in the coal washery at Zeche Zollverein, the former coalmine and coking plant recently designated a world heritage site by the United Nations. A local paper asked its readers to send in 'clean' underwear jokes. The children's theatre was developing a stage version of *The Adventures of Captain Underpants.* In addition, numerous other events were planned by various associations or through private initiative.

At the public library, a lilac banner announced the exhibition for which Moni had been responsible.

Moni let Karo in and took her downstairs to the information desk of the music library.

"He's behind there."

A glass vase filled with pink carnations blocked Karo's view. She pushed it aside, leaned over the desk, and looked down at the dead man lying on a large, black plastic bag.

Early sixties, of rather slight build, thin grey hair under a black woolen cap, a red T-shirt, black jacket, black jeans, red gym shoes. Dark discolored marks on the neck.

"Do you know who he is?"

"No idea. Not one of our regulars. Then at least I would know him by sight."

"Doesn't he have any papers on him?"

"Do you think I would do such a thing as go through his pockets?"

"Well, yes. Being such a mystery fan."

"That is completely different....Anyway, I thought we could hoist him up on this desk chair and then roll him over to geography or art and put him in one of the comfortable armchairs there. Someone is bound to notice him sooner or later. Here."

She handed Karo a pair of turquoise rubber gloves and a large, light blue plastic bag. "I have cut out holes for the head and arms. That way we won't leave any traces or pick up fibers from his clothes. I haven't read Patricia Cornwell for nothing after all. You have to roll up your sleeves."

They pulled the plastic bags over their heads and put on the gloves.

"Great turquoise color," Karo said. "I always have red or yellow ones. Could you find out where I could get these? They look really cool."

"Okay, okay. I'll get a few packs from the broom closet as a bonus to your fee."

"Excellent idea."

Karo bent down over the dead man and took out a calling card from his breast pocket. "Jupp Kniffken, Action Artist, Essen-Borbeck, Stollberg Street "

"Oh, shit," Moni said. "The Beuys of Borbeck."

"What?"

"The husband of a colleague. Frau Kniffken reconstructs the classified catalog of the library's Krupp Collection. I have always heard about her husband, the failed artist."

Moni looked at him, shaking her head. "So that's him. She adored him. This is going to kill her. She is a very sensitive soul."

"Hmm," Karo said. Rule number 11b in the correspondence course *How to Become a Successful Private Detective in Six Weeks* read: "In a murder case the spouse is always the main suspect."

Moni rolled the desk chair into position and got hold of the dead man's legs. When Karo picked him up at the shoulders, his head fell over on the side in a rather unnatural way. Karo lowered the body again.

"You forgot to mention that his neck is broken."

"What?" Moni moved back a few steps. "A broken neck and strangled? Couldn't he have just had a heart attack? Preferably in his own bed. This is a nightmare. Are you sure he has not been poisoned as well?"

Karo looked at her watch. They definitively did not have time for hysterics now. She took the carnations out of the vase and threw the water at Moni's face.

"Karo! Do you want to poison me? There is stay-fresh powder in there."

"Come on. We have to get going."

With a great deal of effort and as much strength as they could muster, accompanied by the rustling swish of the plastic bags, they moved the dead man into a half-way upright position on the desk chair.

"Just as well that there are armrests on the chair," Karo said. "Where to?"

"Over there. Into the geography section."

Karo supported the head. Moni pushed. They

made good progress on the parquet floor. They were just swinging briskly around the corner of a bookshelf when a short piercing scream made them stop dead in their tracks.

Karo turned around. A long, thin, ghost-like figure in a dark flowing gown was moving towards them. A black-gloved hand reached out to them. A whimpering sound came from the figure.

The figure stopped in front of them. "Wha...wha...what are you doing there?"

A black veil was draped over a broad-rimmed hat. Karo could only vaguely see the woman's face.

Moni took a step towards her. "Frau Kniffken? Is that you?"

The woman nodded. "What are you doing with...my husband?"

Moni turned red, then pale. "I...we..." She took Frau Kniffken's hand. Turquoise rubber on black leather. "Frau Kniffken, I am so sorry, your husband unfortunately is, he is dead, I am afraid."

"Of course he is dead. At least I hope so." Frau Kniffken pulled back her hand. "What I want to know is...why you are pushing him around the library like this? And what is this get-up you are wearing? We are not having carnival right now. So, what is going on?"

Moni was smoothing down her plastic smock with both hands. "Well...."

"We had to improvise," Karo said. "I don't think that you—"

"The state prime minister was coming," Moni said. "Perhaps I overreacted."

"Just a minute," Karo said, thinking of rule number 11b.

She raised a turquoise finger. "Just a minute, Frau Kniffken, how did you know that your husband was dead? Why are you already in mourning? In other words, what do you have to do with your husband's death?"

Frau Kniffken paid no attention to Karo. "The prime minister came? That means even more media coverage. And my Jupp was no longer hanging there? Good God," she said, "what a lost opportunity. You will never be able to make up for this. Never!" She started to cry.

"I could not let him just lie there, Frau."

"Hanging there?" Karo called out. "Are you saying he—your husband—was hanging up there? Did you string him up? And you dare to accuse us of—"

Frau Kniffken gave a loud sob.

"Now really, Karo. No way has Frau Kniffken killed her husband. She is in shock. Frau Kniffken, tell her that you have not."

"No," Frau Kniffken said. "I didn't kill him. I could have never done that. I stayed overnight at my cousin's house in Essen-Steele. My Jupp insisted that I should have an alibi. He was always so good to me, so good. Of course he also left a letter announcing his intentions to commit suicide. To be on the safe side. No, I only got him the key for the display case, from your desk drawer, Frau Sydow. And then I let him into the library, after midnight."

She hesitated and wiped a tear from her cheek.

"He was very, very ill, you know, and he didn't want to go on any longer. We talked about him wanting to end his life this morning. In preparing for it, he also thought of the practical details. For instance, he hardly ate anything these last couple of days in order not to, well, you know what I mean. Like those yogis who prepare for self-mummification."

Karo and Moni listened intently, as Frau Kniffken continued to explain.

"And as an artist—he was an action artist, in the early seventies he had quite a good press here in the Ruhr area—but that must have been before your time. In any case, he didn't want to go out like a candle, but with fireworks, with drums rolling, or even better, by causing a scandal. At least a few reports in the press should come out of it. And when I told him about the exhibition, about the items shown, and that the minister of culture would be at the opening, he got all excited and had the idea: he wanted to commit suicide with Madonna's bra."

"Was he a fetishist?"

"Karo, honestly!"

"He was an artist, I already told you," she replied in exasperation. "He was intrigued by the breast as a metaphor. Birth and death. From the mother's breast giving life to a bra giving death, or something like it. I didn't understand it all. But I supported him, as I have always done. And now you have ruined it all. Really! How could you?"

"Frau Kniffken, when Moni—Frau Sydow—found your husband, he was no longer hanging from the balustrade with a bra around his neck for maximum media effect, but was lying on the floor in front of the display case. Presumably the bra fasteners were not strong enough to hold his weight for any length of time."

"I think that's scandalous," Frau Kniffken said. "That bra cannot have been cheap. All those sequins and glittery stones sewn onto it. All done by hand, according to the description in the catalog. Made to measure. And then they skimp on the fasteners."

"Actually, I think—"

"May I suggest," Moni said, "that for now we put him into this armchair and continue our conversation later? The library is opening any minute. Besides, it is getting very hot under these plastic bags."

"Yes," Frau Kniffken said, "My widow's outfit is a bit over the top too for a summer day. Jupp had designed it himself. That's how he was. He thought of everything. In his design he wanted to combine elements from the mourning clothes worn by Queen Victoria and Jackie Kennedy."

"Yes, quite unusual," Moni said. "Perhaps it will help, if you turn the veil back across the hat and leave your face exposed? Yes, like that it should be less sticky. Now all you need is a little bit of lipstick. A serious cherry red. Then you would look perfect."

"We either push him along now, or I leave," Karo said.

"One moment! Frau Sydow could you put Jupp in the art section? There is an armchair there as well. It's only a few meters more, and it would be so much more fitting, don't you think? I will check if there is a monograph on Joseph Beuys; he could be reading that—I mean, have it on his lap. Because he greatly admired Beuys, my Jupp did, yes? And then I will call the press, they must be over in the Haus der Technik right now listening to Germaine Greer. Oh, would one of you have a lipstick for me, perhaps? For the photographs later on."

Frau Kniffken rushed off. Karo and Moni

followed her with Jupp.

Jupp never received the media attention hoped for, but the grieving widow, Frau Kniffken, was awarded the honor of announcing the winner of the underwear joke contest; which was determined by the visitors of the first Essen Lingerie Festival.

The contributor, Frau A. from E., pointed out that the joke dated from the fifties or early sixties when black underwear was considered, at least by the working class people in the Ruhr area, very risqué.

After having been married for twenty-four years, the sex life of a couple in Gladbeck had gone stale. The wife wants to put some vim back into her marriage and was told by a girl friend to be bold and invest in some black underwear. She goes off to buy black panties and a black lace brassiere, which, according to the sales lady, would restore ardour even to the most listless of husbands.

When she came home, her husband, as always, is sitting on the sofa, reading the newspaper. Wearing only her new lingerie she leans against the doorframe and gives a little cough. He looks up and asks: "Something happen to Grandma?"

STORY NINE

THE GOOD OLD DAYS
by Paul D. Marks

In the good old days, the Club Alabam down on Central Avenue near downtown L.A. was the place to be. Cab Calloway and Duke Ellington jammed there when they were in town stayin' at the Dunbar Hotel, not too far away. You know the good old days I'm talking about, the days when the brothers and sisters couldn't stay at just any hotel. When, in some parts of the country, there were colored drinking fountains and white drinking fountains, colored entrances to restaurants, that's if they allowed colored folk in at all. The days when Billie Holiday sang about strange fruit hanging from Southern trees.

You know, the good old days when the Booker 'Boom Boom' Taylor Orchestra, really a small big band, played the Alabam quite often. The Boom Boom Orchestra was a bunch of black dudes—colored dudes back then—with one white dude named Bobby Saxon on the piano. Man could that dude wail on the eighty-eights.

The white folk would come down to the Alabam to live dangerously. To mingle with the coloreds. Slumming. For one of them, a beautiful bottle-blonde with movie star looks and cherry lips, it was a little too dangerous. Her body was found in the middle of the dance floor with a .32 slug in her. A faggot gun, Magis, the detective in charge, had said, since it was of such small caliber.

Everyone wondered how she could have been wasted right in front of all the people in the club. Magis figured with all the dancing and blaring music, and the gun being such a small caliber, that it would have been possible to shoot it off without anyone paying any real mind to it.

Her name was Vera Lear, and it may have been a small bullet but it ruined her white party dress, unless you liked the Rorschach pattern the blood made spinning out in all directions from the entry wound. Her hair was matted together like a homeless dog that'd been out in the rain too long. Several people stood over the body, and the cops ordered them not to leave.

Magis was most interested in her boyfriend Tom Davies, her brother Jared, Booker and the other band members, and a colored gal, Regina, the cigarette girl, who seemed to show an inordinate amount of interest in the corpse. But everyone in the joint was a suspect, from the busboys to the bartenders, the black folk and slumming whites. Everyone was equal at this moment in time.

Magis looked like something out of a gangster movie with his fedora, wide lapel coat, and a butt hanging from his mouth.

"Who's he tryin' to be?" Booker whispered to Bobby as they waited to be questioned, along with all the other patrons and employees of the Alabam. "Humphrey Bogart."

Bobby laughed.

"What's so funny?" Magis turned, sneering at Bobby. "You always laugh when someone's murdered?"

"Don't you laugh to relieve the tension?" Bobby snapped back in his soft, melodic voice.

Magis walked over to Bobby, put his arm around the white musician's shoulder and walked him out of the room, into a cramped storage room that smelled of ammonia. Several uniformed officers and plain clothes dicks kept an eye on the gathered crowd. Magis stood Bobby in the shadows, the only light winding its way in from the Alabam's main room. Magis lit another butt with the end of the one going in his mouth and Bobby hoped the ammonia wasn't combustible. He dropped the butt on the floor of the storage room, took his sweet time about crushing it out. Bobby put his foot on it, mashing it into the floor.

"What'd you do that for?"

"If you burn down the club you'll lose all your evidence."

"Tell you the truth, if it wasn't some white gal I wouldn't give a damn. And that leads me to my first question, what the hell are you doing here playing with the colored crowd?"

Bobby didn't want to antagonize Magis. Why make trouble for himself? Land in jail? To what end? He told the cop the truth, he liked the way they played and, besides, he couldn't get a gig with a white band. That satisfied the detective, who let on that he thought Booker was the prime suspect. He told Bobby to go home. Bobby left via the back door.

On a good day, Bobby could see the Hollywoodland sign from his green and white tiled bathroom window. The tile formed little Egyptian pyramids in the art deco fashion of the day. He stood there now, staring out at the night sky, breathing in the cool jacaranda-scented night air from the open window. The window was always open—it wouldn't close. Luckily it didn't rain much in L.A. and when it did, Bobby put a towel on the sill to soak up the water.

Bobby dragged on a cigarette of his own, Viceroy, the only brand he smoked. The hot jazz sounds of Benny Goodman blitzed into the bathroom from the radio in the living room. Bobby turned from the window to the mirror on the medicine cabinet. He looked at his smooth face, the charcoal gray fedora, the purple shirt with the white tie and wide lapelled jacket. It was the image of cool he wanted to project.

He took the fedora off, setting it on the edge of the tub, and ran his fingers through his short cropped hair. He took the jacket off and draped it across the tub. He'd get a hanger from the bedroom in a few minutes to hang the jacket and shirt from the shower curtain rod, then let the tub steam up so he wouldn't have to send them out to the laundry just yet.

With the tie and shirt off, he removed his undershirt and looked at his chest, his breasts. The breasts of a woman, a small breasted woman, but a woman nonetheless. Because Bobby was a woman through and through, born Roberta. But no band, colored or white, would have a woman except as a canary, a singer. And Bobby didn't want to sing, she wanted to wail on the eighty-eights, so she did what she had to do. She became a man for all intents and purposes. Living like this didn't do much for her love life, but it did everything for the love of her life, music. It was a tradeoff she had to make and one that was well worth it.

Smoke curlicued through the highly burnished wooden booths at Musso and Frank's, like a snake slithering through the trees of its jungle home. Bobby sat in a booth nursing a scotch, water back. Booker entered, wearing a navy blue pinstripe suit with a white carnation in the lapel. His marcelled hair shined under the lights. Several sets of green and blue eyes turned to look at him, but no one said anything. Musso's was one of the few white places in L.A. that a colored man could walk into, even eat in. He sat in the booth across from Bobby, ordering a gin and tonic from the waiter.

"Thanks for taking the time to meet me, Bobby." He drummed his fingers on the table, tapping the silverware in a nerve-jangling 8/4 beat.

"Am I gonna turn the boss down?" Bobby said, hinting at a smile.

"You turn me down every time I ask you to go out with my sister. I suppose it is impolitic in this city in this day and age."

"That's not why I do it. I just don't think it's right to date the boss's sister." Bobby's voice was a little deeper than it needed to be. But he was making a point. "What if something went wrong? She'd get P.O.'d at me, and I'd be out of a gig."

"I wouldn't do that to you. You bang the best keyboards I ever heard."

"Still, it's better not to take a chance."

The waiter brought Booker's drink. He took a long swig. Then another. There wasn't much left in the glass after that. His eyes bored into Bobby. They were like steel rivets drilling into him. That was one of Booker's specialties, he grabbed people with his eyes.

Once he turned them on you either you couldn't look away or you couldn't do anything but look away. Bobby could take it, at least for short periods of time.

Booker's eyes were more intense than usual today. Something was up.

"I think they're gonna pinch me," he said, "for that white lady's murder. They need to pin it on someone. Why not on the colored band leader? On the man with Mesmer's eyes."

"You really think they want to pin it on you 'cause you're black?" Bobby sipped his drink, pretending to enjoy the taste.

"They got no leads. I got no alibi, lessin' you can alibi me."

"Why me?"

"You're white."

"You think that will be enough?"

"Sure will."

"We're not all brothers under the skin, you know, white people. Detective Magis and I are about as far removed from each other as two people can be. Besides, I'm a musician in a colored band. That'll be a strike against me. I'm not saying I won't do it, just trying to give you a dose of reality."

"I work in an unreal business. I create musical dreams for people to slide away on. It's better than takin' the Horse. But I still got more'n enough reality for one person's lifetime."

Bobby asked Booker where he had been when the murder had occurred. Two bands had played that night, alternating sets. Booker's orchestra had been off when Vera was killed and he claimed to be out in the alley having a smoke. But he couldn't tell the cops he'd been alone, smoking reefer. That kind of confession would get him another kind of bust. Bobby agreed to alibi Booker, hoping he wasn't the killer. Besides, maybe this would get him in good with the boss, get him a raise. Maybe some day it would get his name on the posters alongside Booker's.

Bobby knew Booker had come up the hard way, from the mean streets of Birmingham, where a black man better not be seen with a white woman. Hell, sometimes he'd better not be seen period. There was a rumor going 'round that Booker had killed a white boy once, when he was about sixteen. The boy had tried to rape his sister, the same sister that wanted to date Bobby. Booker had taken him out to one of the mills outside of town and bashed his head in with a chunk of iron ore. Booker never talked about the story. It just went around the band and the folks who came to see them. Bobby believed the story. But that didn't mean he believed Booker had killed Vera. Why would he?

La Tempesta was a raging, raving piano-dominated piece that Bobby had seen Freddy Martin's band do at the Coconut Grove. But now it was Bobby and Booker's and their band's turn to wail on it. By the time the number was over, Bobby had lost three pounds in sweat and his hair glistened in it. The rest of the band lost a pound and a half each. The audience in the smoky club was on its feet stomping and clapping, whistling and yelling. Bobby was out of breath. Time for a break, even though the band's break wouldn't come for another twenty minutes.

He had been in the alley behind the club only a minute or two, about to light up a coffin nail, when Magis came out. Magis stuck his hand in his coat pocket—to get a gun, handcuffs? No, a Lucky Strike. He put it between his lips and Bobby offered him his lighter, which Magis refused, preferring to strike a match on his shoe like he'd seen done in the movies, no doubt.

"Alibi Ike," Magis said, exhaling a plume of gray smoke. Bobby still hadn't lit his butt. He rolled the lighter in his fingers. "Good number. Hot."

"Thanks, Detective." They talked about the statement Bobby had given the cops earlier in the day, backing up Booker's story about being in the alley for a smoke.

"You'd better hope that we don't find out otherwise. I don't think you'd like our jails, nice as we try to maintain them. A pretty boy like you wouldn't last very long in there."

"Thanks for your concern, Detective." Bobby finally lit his cigarette. "How's the case going?" There was only the slightest hint of scorn in his voice. He didn't know if Magis picked up on it or not. Of course, he couldn't afford to land in jail, go through a body search and have them find out he wasn't what he was pretending to be. And if they didn't find out until later he would really be in trouble for the time he was in jail. He had often thought about going to a gym, there were several in Hollywood, and learning to box. As it was, he knew he couldn't do much to take care of himself, other than jam his tuning fork into someone's eye.

"Y'know," Magis said, drawing deep on his Lucky Strike, "I was thinking, if two people were involved they might be able to alibi each other."

"Interesting point. But first you need a motive,

don't you? What do you think the motive is in this case?"

"I don't know, what are the usual motives; blackmail, money, jealousy. There's also rage, hate, love, love-turned-to-hate. A spurned lover. There's really not that many motives under God's yellow sun."

He smiled at Bobby through a clenched mouth, with the cigarette dangling there, turned and walked back into the club. Bobby drew on his cigarette, hacking out a large, black, smoke-filled cough and threw the thing on the ground, crushing it under his Florsheim shoe. He waited a moment before heading inside.

Taking his place on stage, he joined the band on the number they were already halfway through. Booker sidled up to him.

"What'd that cop want?"

"Just seeing if I'd break. Don't look so worried."

Booker's face relaxed. Almost sagged with relief. The band boogied on. Booker was about to return to his spot center stage when Bobby asked, "Did you know her?"

"What?"

Bobby didn't think Booker hadn't heard him. "Did you know her?"

"I seen her around the club a few times. She like to come on down here an' go slummin' with us po' coloreds." Booker put on his best sharecropper's accent.

"That's it? You didn't know her any better than that?"

Booker shook his head and ambled to center stage in time with the music. With so much to lose, Bobby decided to help the police find the killer. He hoped it wasn't Booker. The gig with his band was a good one and paid pretty well for this kind of work. He didn't want to have to go auditioning for another band. Sure he had a reputation of sorts with the locals now, but he was comfortable here. And if he joined a road band...look out. He'd have to share a hotel room with another band member or two. And how could he keep his secret then?

No, the best thing to do was help the police find the killer and pray it was someone other than Booker.

Jared Lear was a medium sized man, about five feet ten inches tall. His shoulders were broad and the suits of the time made them look broader. His hair was black, his skin milk white. It made for an interesting look. The piercing blue eyes didn't hurt either. Bobby knew him as someone to say hello to in the club. Jared's number was in the book and Bobby had no trouble setting up an appointment to meet him.

Bobby had also known Jared's sister. Vera had frequented the club almost every weekend, even more often than Jared. She was a looker in her Oleg Cassini look-alike dresses and Max Factor eyes. Those eyes had expressed desire for Bobby at one time, until Bobby made it clear that he was otherwise engaged.

Jared's apartment building on Fountain—the good part of town—had turrets in each of the second floor corners. It looked like a castle out of a Hollywood movie. Bobby wondered if there would be nothing behind the door of the building when he entered, another movie facade in a land of fake fronts, something out of West's *Day of the Locusts*.

It wasn't a fake front, at least not in the literal sense. But the hall carpet was faded and musty. Yellowish light filtered in through the downed shade at the end of the hall. Dust mites danced on the light. The building must have been expensive to live in and, for the money they paid, the tenants deserved better care.

One of those turrets was Jared's living room. Bobby sat at a small, round table in the turret, drinking a cup-a-joe across the table from Jared. It was three in the afternoon and he was still in his pajamas under the satin robe he wore. The apartment was clean, as if it was, indeed, a movie set. Bobby's eyes scanned the room.

Bobby took in the Gainsborough prints on the walls. The sterling silver cigarette case meant to impress on the coffee table and the crossed dueling swords and coat of arms over the fireplace meant to intimidate. The strategically placed books by strategically important authors, from Marx to Hitler. Freud to Rand. Hemingway to Pearl S. Buck.

"I don't get it, Bob, you helping the coppers? Not that I mind. We need all the help we can get to find Vera's killer."

"I'm not doing it to help them, but to help the band out. It's all very disruptive with the police nosing around day and night."

Jared exited into his bedroom, calling out to Bobby. "I'm afraid there's not much I can tell you about that night that you don't already know."

"Who'd you and she come to the club with?" Bobby poked around. Nothing unusual. A couple decks of cards, some magazines, Life, Photoplay. Plane tickets to Mexico with a phone number written next to them. Bobby wrote the number down, though he wasn't sure why.

"It was a whole group of people. There were

seven or eight of us, maybe more. It's hard to recall now. I was a little tight, if you know what I mean," Jared said, returning to the living room, wearing a black armband on his white shirtsleeve. He shot Bobby a knowing look, the look of those who've seen one too many a bathroom stall from their knees. It didn't mean much to Bobby as he didn't drink much, and then only to fit in with the rest of the band. To that end he'd smoke reefer with them on occasion, but avoided it when he could.

"Anyone in particular?" Bobby said. Jared's eyes opened wide, his face darting into a quizzical expression. "You know, was she seeing anyone? Or was there anyone who had it out for her, spurned lover, that kind of thing?" As he said it, Magis' words echoed in his mind, the usual motives: blackmail, rage, jealousy. Money.

"Everyone liked Vera, party girl."

"Maybe someone she didn't want to party with."

"No. I can't think of anyone. But if you want to know who she was seeing, his name was Tom Davies. Lives not too far from here." He wrote an address down on a piece of paper.

Bobby offered his condolences again, as he had upon arriving, and left staring at the address on Mansfield. To get there, he drove east on Beverly Boulevard. Bobby would normally have to take Sunset, Melrose, or Santa Monica to go east, or in this case he would have stayed on Fountain, but it was closed for some kind of road work, so he was detoured south.

He liked to avoid Beverly as he would have to pass Alta Vista and Beverly. He had grown up half a block north of Beverly on Alta Vista. It was a one story

Spanish Colonial Revival house, with an arched portico leading to the front door. The color was a gray bordering on mauve, at least that's how he remembered it. He slowed as he approached the intersection. The car behind him honked furiously. Bobby could see the man in his mirror animatedly yelling and flailing his arms. He put his left hand out the window and signaled the irate driver to go around. It took him long enough to get the message.

After he passed, Bobby swerved north and drove up Alta Vista. Half a block north of Beverly he slowed the car to a halt in the middle of the street. There was little to no traffic on a street like this, and if anyone came he'd pull over. For now, his eyes were fixed on the one story stucco house across the road. The color had a little more plum in it than he had remembered, otherwise it was the same, down to the large hedge in front where he, uh, she and her friends had played Secret Passage, a game they made up in which going behind the hedge could take you anywhere in the world, at least in your imagination. But for them it was real enough. It always was for kids, wasn't it?

And the Secret Passage was the place she liked the best, even when her friends weren't around to play with. It was her refuge from the world. Her escape when she heard her father yelling at her mother. When she wished her mother would scoop her up in her arms and take her away, via the Secret Passage, to a land of gentle breezes and palm trees—but not like those here in L.A. A land she had seen in a Jon Hall movie once.

She didn't know when she had seen the movie that the land of exotic palms was only a few miles away on a studio backlot. For her it was as real as the blood trickling down her mother's nose after her father hit her.

At the same time, she admired her father's power. It was awesome. Dynamic. Potent. And seemingly all-encompassing. She envied that kind of power and wished her mother had possessed even one tenth of it. She hadn't seen her mother or father in several years. As far as she knew they were still together. As her mother had said, that was their way of relating. It worked for them.

Bobby put the car in gear and rolled forward, turning around. Getting back on Beverly Boulevard, he headed for Mansfield. Davies was home when Bobby knocked on his duplex door. Like Jared, he worked as a movie extra. Unlike Jared, his apartment was a mess, newspapers from three days ago scattered here and there. Unfinished food. A sock here, a pair of pants draped over a chair there. He didn't look happy to see someone at his door. Bobby wondered, is it me, or would it have been anyone?

Bobby introduced himself. Davies said he didn't recognize him at first but that he'd been to the Alabam and knew Booker's band.

"I don't know what happened," he said, a defensive tone infesting his voice.

"I went to the bar for a few minutes. When I returned, she was dead. I really don't know any more than that."

Bobby knew he was an amateur at detecting. But he'd seen enough Hollywood movies on the subject to feel he wasn't a total novice. Unless Davies could back up that alibi for the moment of the murder, it might or might not be true. And he couldn't back it up. He said he'd told it to the police and they questioned the bartender, other patrons, and no one could place Davies at the bar at any specific time.

The main question on Bobby's mind was why was Davies' apartment a mess, the neglect of a distraught boyfriend, or the outward manifestation of a guilty mind?

Bobby could have interviewed Booker next, but what good would that do? He was too smooth an operator and would have both seen through it and been able to talk his way out of it. Instead, he got Regina's address and went to her apartment. It was small and dark and not in a very good part of town. Bobby wasn't too thrilled to park several doors up the street and have to walk to the apartment on foot after dark.

Regina knew who he was, offered him a lemonade spiked with gin in a chipped coffee mug. Bobby explained why he was there.

"Sure I wanna kill the bitch. Why not? She's screwin' that white boy and my man, Booker, too."

"I didn't know Booker and you were an item." Maybe Bobby wasn't as close to Booker and the band as he'd thought. He eyeballed Regina's apartment. Small. Tidy. Cheap furniture and obviously cheap glasses. Either that or she kept the fine china for the King of England's visits.

"We ain't no item. We like glued together. Sometimes we drift apart, but we always come home to each other. You might say I'm Booker's backstreet girl, he don't want the world knowin' 'bout us."

Regina stopped long enough to catch her breath,

then continued, "But I ain't no jealous woman scorned. An' if I did it, you can be sure I wouldn't do it in front of a whole crowd-a people. And I'd use a bigger gun, too."

Bobby smiled at that, remembering Magis' comments about the pistol. "Whoever did it wasn't seen in that crowd."

"Maybe that's smart then. Maybe it's best to do it in a group, and then nobody sees or hears it."

"What else can you tell me?"

"That bitch was pregnant with my man's baby. Shoulda been mine." Regina blurted it out without thinking. It might have been the gin in her lemonade or maybe she was a little more jealous—and angry—than she liked to let on.

Bobby tried to conceal the look of surprise on his face. Pregnant with Booker's child. That was news. He didn't know what else to say though. Regina was either a damn good actress, playing the angry woman who's above killing or she was enough of a psycho to have talked herself out of any notion she could have done it. Bobby had no more questions. He thanked Regina for the lemonade and split.

Bobby was late for the gig that night. Not late enough for show time, but he didn't make the rehearsal jam backstage that Booker liked to have before the first set. Bobby rushed in, taking off his street coat, putting on the monogrammed band jacket that all the band members wore. Booker eyed him, came over. He thought the boss was going to chew him out.

Booker grabbed Bobby by the sleeve, pulled him to a corner of the dressing room. "I heard a rumor that Vera was pregnant," Booker whispered.

"You think that ties in with her murder?" Bobby played along.

"Dunno. Just thought I'd pass it on."

Bobby had to wonder why it was important for Booker to feed him that bit of info, er, gossip. If he was the father, he might know and he might have wanted to get rid of Vera. But why tell Bobby in either case?

Bobby was a little off tempo during the set that night. His heart and gut weren't in the music. He played La Tempesta, but it was more like a mild breeze than a tempest. He kept running it over in his mind. A jealous woman might have killed Vera if the jealous woman's man had made her pregnant. The possibilities were endless. What motives might the other suspects have?

Booker? Booker could be loose, reckless. He might not care if his gal was pregnant, unless she was a white woman. Maybe Vera was blackmailing him. And Davies. He might not like the idea of his girlfriend getting knocked up by a black man. That was motive enough.

When the set was over, Bobby ducked out before anyone could catch him. The drive uptown was uneventful. But the walk to his car had been less so. As he'd walked out of the club, throngs of black and white-skinned people were waiting to get in, and a carload of white teenagers drove by. "Nigger lover!" one had yelled. If Bobby really was a he, if he really had the power his father had, he would have taken off after them. If only she were a man. But she wasn't, so she headed uptown.

Still, those boys had given her an idea. As had Magis's words: hate. What could make someone hate

Vera enough to kill her? Bobby stopped at a payphone, dialed the number he had written down.

Instead of going home, Bobby swung by Jared's. From the street, he could see the lights on in his turret. He knocked on the door. Jared looked surprised to see Bobby, but let him in. He wore his robe over slacks and shiny wingtips. Bobby could see that he was wearing a T shirt under the robe. He smelled good. Like he'd just slapped on a gallon of aftershave. Old Spice?

"What can I do for you, Bobby? I'm sort of in a hurry."

Bobby knew he should have called Magis. Should have, but hadn't. He wanted to do this on his own. If he did, he hoped, he might gain some of his father's power.

"Gotta date?"

Jared hesitated. His fingers drummed the little table in the turret. He didn't have much rhythm. Could never have cut it with Booker.

"I would have thought you'd be in mourning for your sister." Bobby bore down on Jared with his eyes. His heart raced.

"I am in mourning. But that doesn't mean I should stay home all the time and cry in my beer." He stood up, towering over Bobby, who also stood up. Jared still towered over him.

"Why'd you do it, Jared?" It took everything Bobby could muster to get the words out and once they were, he was exhausted, as if he'd just played La Tempesta ten times in a row.

"Do what?" The impatience in his voice lashed out like a whip in Bobby's direction. Jared moved into the bedroom. To get a gun? Bobby followed. Jared took off the robe, put on a white dress shirt and tie. He put the black armband on the shirt sleeve.

Bobby was scared. His heart pounded a staccato tattoo. It was too late to turn back now. Jared could kill him. After all, he'd killed his own sister. But if he wormed out now, he wouldn't be able to live with himself. "Was it 'cause she was dating an actor?" Bobby knew that wasn't the answer. He wanted Jared to come up with it on his own. Jared straightened his tie and put on a pair of gold cufflinks.

"Or maybe it's cause she was pregnant by a...." Bobby hesitated. The word was hard coming but he knew the force it carried. Knew it would stab Jared like a sharp knife. "Nigger."

Jared's head snapped in Bobby's direction. It startled him, so he took a step back.

"How did you know?" Jared said, more matter-of-factly than Bobby would have imagined.

"The tickets to Mexico. The phone number. I called it. I know enough Spanish to figure out what they were talking about. Why would you need to know about Mexican abortions? Either you got someone pregnant or someone you know was pregnant. But maybe they didn't want to have the procedure."

Jared looked Bobby in the eye, piercing the musician's eyes with his own intense stare. "Whose side are you on, Bobby?" He moved in on Bobby.

"She was your sister." Bobby stood his ground. "I don't get it. You're down at the club twice a week, jumpin' and jivin'. Enjoying their music, hanging with the coloreds all the time."

"Hanging with them's one thing, lettin' one in the family's another."

"It would have been your niece or nephew."

"It wouldn't-a-been my anything. And, as you can see, it still won't." He smiled an evil smile. Bobby stepped back. Jared launched on him, tearing the tie from his neck and throwing it around Bobby's. He jerked Bobby to the ground, jamming his knee in the pianist's belly—better than breaking the hands, Bobby thought, as they tumbled to the floor. Bobby gasped for air. He'd heard that one sees a movie of their life roll by in the moments before death. He saw no movie. He gathered all the strength he possessed. Jared continued yanking the tie tighter.

Bobby's field of vision blurred. He pulled everything he had together and kneed Jared between the legs. Hard. Jared fell off Bobby, groaning in pain. Bobby lurched to his feet and stood over him, wobbly. When Jared started to get to his knees, Bobby kicked him again.

"For good measure," he said, as Jared went down again. Bobby reached for the phone. Dialed. "Detective Magis, please."

Magis arrived at Jared's apartment a few minutes later, to find Jared still writhing on the floor. Of course, he denied killing his sister. Magis lit a smoke. He kicked Jared in the small of the back for the hell of it.

"I thought maybe you wouldn't want the killer to be white," Bobby said.

"You underestimate me, my friend. I may've said something before to lead you on one way or another, but I don't give a damn who did it, colored, white, or green. I do give a damn for the law, believe it or not."

Magis had a way with words, Bobby thought.

The detective clapped Bobby on the shoulder with a beefy hand. "Maybe you should think about joining the force. You're a good man, Bobby."

Bobby grinned.

STORY TEN

FLOATERS
by Patricia Gulley

A momentary feeling of being in free fall woke me. The sensation was followed by a mournful groan as the house rocked forward and met the deck rolling backward. My eyes flew open with the usual disorientation, and I saw a parade of ink black waves rolling in from the river, their crests reflecting the golden light of the full moon.

A few broke noisily against my deck while the rest made their way to shore. A large boat must have passed by, not minding the five-mile-an-hour speed limit.

I had come out to watch the glorious gold, pink, and apricot sunset that made summer feel like a tangible treasure. It needed to be savored in this land of gloom where it rained ten months out of every year. I couldn't believe I'd fallen asleep and missed it.

Before the wake was finished, the house and deck knocked together again, and one bump felt like something other than water had hit. Maybe a log, nothing tree-size like the ones used to float the houses and decks, but a-two or three-footer that would make a nice addition to my deck décor. Once it dried out and stopped smelling, of course.

I struggled up from my comfy deck chair pulling and tugging at my blouse and capri pants and hoped my little snooze hadn't been embarrassing for me while hilarious for my neighbors. I walked to the edge of the deck and looked down into the water. Something was bobbing there, but it wasn't a log. On closer inspection, it appeared to be a wad of cloth. It was too dark to see clearly or reach down; it might be some irresponsible boater's garbage.

Every floating homeowner keeps a broom on deck for cleaning up spider webs. I used mine to poke at the object and, if it was garbage, shift it to shore where moorage maintenance would haul it away in the morning. Whatever it was, it felt soft and mushy, and I began to worry about my broom. It had to be a bag of something bad, so I pushed it to the corner of the deck where I could sweep it around and shove it toward shore.

I didn't put the right English on my push and it hit the corner and bounced away. I had to slap at it to keep it from heading back into the river, and that caused it to bob furiously like a cork and roll over. Two lifeless eyes in a bloated face stared up at me.

I screamed and tripped over my feet backing away. Luckily, my neighbors, Janie and Wes, had been sitting in their gazebo the whole time, watching, and good-humoredly offering helpful instructions and quips as I'd smacked at the thing with my broom. Their deck was several feet shorter than mine and hadn't been hit as hard with the waves. They rushed to the edge of their deck and Janie, who carries her cell phone everywhere, was on to 911 and island security in a flash.

The police took a little longer. Jantzen Beach on Hayden Island in the Columbia River is the last exit off I-5 before crossing the bridge and border between Oregon and Washington. Several floating home communities existed on the slough side of the island that liked to be called North Portland Harbor. Just another example of the strong neighborhood feel, no matter the location, that is very much a part of Portland's public policy.

It surprised me that the body floated into our little inlet between two rows; dead things tended to float away in the swift waters of the Columbia on its way to the Pacific Ocean. The men of the neighborhood secured the poor thing with the help of the harbor patrol. The police had to get through our security gate, but they finally presented themselves and the questioning began.

Everyone on two rows came out to see what was going on, making a long night for the police.

Wes and Janie said it was a tugboat that had passed by pushing a barge of gravel that caused the wake. They hadn't observed anyone tossing anything overboard. Wes voiced his opinion that the body couldn't have just been killed and dumped in the river. He said it looked like it had been in the water for a while. The police offered no opinion or answers to our questions or statements.

I stayed up to watch the late news, hoping the TV people had learned something in their inscrutable way, but they hadn't.

I'm a retired travel agent, but still work as a tour escort for a local operator of short tours in Washington and Oregon. They also do Christmas at the Empress in Victoria BC, but I don't work that one, too much family here in Portland to be away at that time of year. I do escort day tours to Oregon wine country, Tillamook Cheese Factory and Seattle Mariner Games. We do overnighters to the United Tribes casino in Grand Ronde, whale watching in

Lincoln City and Florence to see the Sea Lion Caves and Heceta Head Lighthouse. We do two-nighters to Ashland Shakespearean Theater with Crater Lake and Leavenworth for the lighting ceremony and pre-Christmas shopping.

After my divorce, a life-long attraction to beach houses that I never wanted to spend just a vacation in became more than fulfilled with a floating home. Plus I'd vowed never to mow or do yard work again, my ex claimed to be the gardener while I got stuck with the grunt work. So I do about ten escorts a year. The small salary and tips help supplement my income and support my travel fund for longer cruises or tours abroad. I guess you could say I loved my work and would miss the excitement of going places if I had a stay-at-home retirement.

Anyway, finding a body like that should have been enough excitement for one lifetime, but you know the fates and their sense of humor. The next night my friend Barbara, who lives in the first house on our row, (there are six) found another one bobbing between the main walkway and her deck. We went through the same routine with the harbor patrol and the police.

The night after that, two policemen watched from Barb's (house one) and my (house four) decks, but nothing floated our way. Our back decks faced the front of the houses on the next row over. Ruthie, another friend that lives on that row, came home from a date and leaned against the metal railing to ask if we'd found another one yet. She glanced down before turning away from our negative response and was waving her arms and screaming in seconds. No jumping the fence between houses or yards here, the cops had to run from the decks to the front of our houses to get on the walkway for our row, turn on to the main walkway, then turn into Ruthie's row to see what had scared her. Sure enough, it was another body.

On the fourth night, we had a cop on every deck, along both rows and on the main walkway between the two rows. Chaos broke out when three more bodies bobbed up and floated into the open water between the two rows. Where were they coming from? No boats were going by, no one was dumping anything into the river from the opposite side of the slough or from any of the decks. With the exception of the end house (number six) everyone was on their deck. Six had been recently sold, and we were told they would be weekenders not permanent residents. It was only Thursday.

The cops called in more cops, the harbor patrol, detectives and the forensic people. The TV news helicopters circled while reporters tried to gain access to our gated community. When they were turned away, they set up their news vans on the opposite bank, and that caused a mass of gawkers to arrive. They made the crowds that formed along Marine Drive for the Fort Vancouver fireworks look like a small gathering of friends. If there had been any forensic clues to be found over there, they were trampled away by campers, who had to be from the same gene pool that produced the lunch-eaters at hangings.

By Saturday, my kitchen cabinet doors were swinging open with the roll from so many boaters going by trying to see what was going on. Harbor patrol had its hands full. We have one hundred and twenty houses in the moorage and the police had kept the foot traffic of owners off the two rows right from the start. I kept track of all this from my front storm door as I watched for the new owners of house six to arrive.

Every row has a captain, and I'm it for this one. One of my yearly duties is to drop dye into the toilets of every house, flush, turn on two sink faucets full blast, and run out to watch the honey pot pump into the sewer lines. If the pots have leaks, the dye makes them very visible. I'd done everyone the weekend before except the end house. It didn't seem very important considering what was happening, on the other hand no one was rushing to keep me posted or updated on the progress of the investigation, so I went back to my daily routine.

I kept an eye on the ramp that led down from the bank and parking lot and didn't notice one of the detectives walking towards me from the direction of the slough until he stepped onto my deck. He wore a business suit and was my age or maybe even younger. He didn't smile, just flipped open a badge case.

"Detective Andy Hayden, and yes, I'm related," he said. Since we lived on Hayden Island, everyone must have been asking him if he was descended from one of the pioneering families. Related meant he was a webfoot. Not me, imported twenty years ago and still having fun teasing the born-again-everything locals.

"What can I do for you, detective?" I asked and added, "No, I haven't seen the people on the end arrive yet." I can play the anticipated question game too.

"Arrive yet?" he asked, surprised I'd guessed what he wanted.

I gave him a clipped description of what I knew. "New owners from Hood River I've been told. Boaters, who will only be using it for weekends and maybe a few full weeks in the summer. Don't know them by sight, but any strangers turning down the row might be them."

My speech was recorded in his little notebook, so I also explained why I was watching for them.

"And you say they weren't here last weekend?"

I shook my head and he looked back at the house as though worried. I asked him why.

His eyes narrowed into a suspicious frown as he stared down the row, thinking. He said, "An empty house with so many bodies floating around is one of those things that makes my scalp crawl." Then he smiled briefly as though it suddenly occurred to him that he might be scaring me, and added, "Just a cop thing."

Cop thing my foot, he was right, and I suddenly wanted desperately to get into that house. I grabbed my bottle of dye and signaled for the detective to follow me.

"I know you have to worry about warrants and all that, but I'm a row captain with a duty to perform and a sense of responsibility for the houses and people on my row." I said this while trying to look downright upstanding and efficient as I grabbed his arm and dragged him on to Wes and Janie's porch. I gave him a small smile to reassure him and banged on their door.

Janie looked out, all interested. "Janie, do you have a key to the week-enders house?"

"Oh sure, from when Norma and Gordon lived there. Oh, do you want to do the test? Let me get it."

Detective Hayden could hardly believe how easily he'd gained access to the house. While he looked around, I told him I was going to do my tests. Fine with him, it was the legitimate reason for being on the premises. I turned on the kitchen and bathroom tap, but before pouring the dye had to locate the honey pot, because unlike most it wasn't in plain view on the front or side of the house. Some owners put them under their decks, so I went out to look for a trap door. The deck ran the length of the left side of the house and faced out to the water. Looking east and west provided a magnificent view of the entire waterway.

There were several boats going in both directions and a few were hovering nearby, trying not to seem obvious. The campers on the opposite side hadn't dwindled, but a lot of nighttime partying had most of them sleeping late into the morning. I found the trap door on the west-end of the deck and got down on my hands and knees to lift it.

There was so much traffic on the water I didn't pay attention to the noise of boat engines, or a slight bump of the house. When I got the door open, I could see it was twice the width of the honey pot and there in the open space beside the tank was another body.

I jumped back ready to shout for the detective and came face to face with a man climbing onto the deck from a cabin cruiser with a tall flying bridge. He stared at me and then down at the body. His hand came out of his pocket holding a gun. "Who are you?" he demanded.

"Your neighbor," I trembled, hoping he was the new owner. "The row captain. I'm doing the honey pot test."

With every word his expression became more panicky. I had a feeling that here was our killer not believing that someone had found his dumpsite so quickly. If he was the new owner, he must have been dumping them for the last two weeks. Why had no one seen him doing it? And why hadn't he seen that some were missing? Had he not realized they wouldn't sink?

I started to raise my hands. His boat was big enough to hide us from the campers' view, but I hoped maybe someone boating up the slough heading west might see me.

"Don't do that," he hissed and then motioned with his gun for me to go back into the house. This was good, but only if the detective wasn't distracted elsewhere.

I was in luck. Not only was the detective waiting with his gun drawn, so were two uniformed policemen.

The gunman gave a yelp when he saw them, dropped his gun and threw up his hands. "I didn't kill anyone, honest, I didn't."

One of the policemen cuffed him, and Detective Hayden read him his rights. When the suspect said he understood his rights, the detective asked, "What's your name?"

"Matthew Sholmes," he choked out between hiccups and sobs. He was young, maybe in his thirties, well-dressed and groomed. "It's my house, and that woman is a trespasser." He blurted this out and nodded towards the gun on the floor. Did he think that was the only trouble he was in?

The name sounded vaguely familiar, but not from hearing it related to the moorage. I passed on thinking about it though to listen to the detective.

"It isn't a normal practice to draw a gun on people, even when you think they are trespassing."

I chimed in with, "He drew the gun when he saw I had the trap door to the honey pot open. I found another body next to the pot."

Detective Hayden sent one of the policemen out to have a look, and asked, "How did you get here?"

Sholmes' face scrunched up in a pained expression and he slumped down into a chair and didn't answer.

"By boat," I answered for him. "It's parked at the west end of the deck, close to the trap door."

The cop, who'd gone out to look, called out that there was indeed another body under the house.

"Take a quick look on board the boat parked there," Hayden yelled back, and turned a raised eyebrow to Sholmes.

He looked resigned and defeated, but still refused to speak.

The policeman came rushing through the sliding glass doors from the deck. "Hayden, there's two more bodies on the boat, and I found this." He handed the detective a brochure.

Hayden took the brochure and looked at it. He was about to respond when he got a call on his cell phone. His responses were "No kidding, really? Yeah, yeah, fits with what we found." He hung up and walked over to Sholmes and held the brochure up. I got a good look at it, and it clicked where I'd seen the name before.

"So, Mr. Sholmes," he said. "I suppose it's not unusual for an undertaker to be in possession of so many bodies, but will you please explain why you were bringing them here by boat and dumping them?"

The Sholmes family had funeral homes all over the state. Matthew was the youngest son. He'd been put in charge of the operations in the town of Hood

River. Unfortunately, he'd run into personal financial problems that he didn't want the family to know about. His brainstorm to cut costs was not to pay for shipping and cremations. He'd get rid of the bodies some other way.

When his wife bought this floating home and didn't want to use it until she had it all properly decorated to her specifications, he knew he had a place to store them for weeks, maybe months. She was known to have walls repainted several times before finally deciding on wallpaper. This would give him time to transport the bodies, a few at a time, down the Columbia River from Hood River at night and dump them through the trap door. He thought the logs under the house would keep them in place. He knew there were quite a few now, so he started bringing cinder blocks to weigh them down so they would sink and the strong undercurrent would eventually take them out to sea. A few cinder blocks were also found on the boat.

Before they took him away, he had a good cry and said his nerves were completely shot. We had no idea how difficult it was sneaking those bodies out of the funeral parlor, onto his boat and then wrestling them into the honey pot space. Even harder was getting the bodies tied up to the cinder blocks through that small opening in the dark. He was positively exhausted.

Well, it wasn't murder, but the detective did say that charges would be brought. There are laws governing the mishandling of corpses, not to mention defrauding the families of the dead.

Needless to say, it was the talk of the moorage for weeks, and it became the best story I told to my busloads of tour participants as we crossed the miles between origination and destination. It was an especially big hit with the mystery tour I helped escort once a year where the participants didn't even know where they were going for three days. I titled it, "The Bodies in the Basement-A Floating Home Version."

STORY ELEVEN

DEATH BY TRIAL AND ERROR
by R. Barri Flowers

She wanted to kill the bloody bastard.

But how?

Run him down with her car?

She could imagine him begging for his life, as he lay wounded in the street, bones broken from head to toe. She would make him suffer before again rolling the car over the damaged goods. And again, until the life had been snuffed out of him.

Perhaps she should lace his chicken noodle soup with cyanide? She would get a great thrill out of seeing him clutch his burning throat in a desperate attempt to relieve his agony. Or roll his eyes from a combination of the poison taking effect and the sheer disbelief of it all. She would dance with delight watching him squirm on the floor as if he had been possessed by the devil himself.

And in that final moment of distress between life and death, she would laugh at him spitefully, the way he surely had been laughing at her for the last six months. Or however long it had been since he'd decided sharing another woman's bed gave him more pleasure and passion than sharing hers.

It was exactly one week ago, as she lay in their

bedroom, that Harrison had told her of his affair. His intonation, usually deep with assurance and rich with confidence, had come across as flat and unrepentant. She felt as if she had been lowered in molten lava. Or told she had a malignant tumor. The pain could not have been any worse.

"What—?" The word shot from her throat like a cannon. She was certain she had misunderstood him. Or even if she understood him correctly, he surely couldn't have meant that which she feared most.

Perhaps he was only playing with her, looking for some sort of reaction. He often liked teasing her, telling her things that would incense her, only to laugh playfully like a schoolboy who had pulled up a schoolgirl's dress merely for the sake of fun and frolic.

She hated this in Harrison, this power he had over her to bring to the brink of tears, to make her feel her whole world was about to collapse, then just as easily make her believe she had the whole world and all its wonderful blessings in the palm of her hand again. With him being her most cherished blessing of all.

Yes, he brought out the best and worst in her, often with merely a gesture, a smile, a frown, a comment, a non-comment, or some other manner of communication that could only exist between a husband and wife.

She looked at him, standing in the entryway of the bedroom, as if to support the frame of rich mahogany. Or the alabaster walls on each side, decorated with framed photographs of them during happier times when all seemed as if it were meant to be.

For just an instant, it was as if she had gone back in time some two decades earlier when she first met Harrison Kincaid and fell in love almost the moment he flashed her his megawatt smile. He was tall, dark, and alluring. His build was solid muscle, as if made to her most ideal specifications. Raven hair stood atop his head in tiny curls, and perfectly suited his square-jawed face. His eyes were a dark shade of gray. They were the type of eyes that penetrated to the depths of your soul when he fixed you with them. She thought he was easily the most handsome man she'd ever seen.

That much had not changed in all these years, she admitted, if only to herself.

It had been a childless marriage, borne as much from genetic mismatches as the decision to forgo having children in favor of their careers and each other.

He had gotten up, careful not to wake her, and dressed as if it was just another day in the life of Harrison Kincaid: author, pilot, lecturer, investor, and major league asshole. She wondered how long he had stood there watching her, replaying his revelation over and over in his mind, trying to think of how best to let her down easily. For all Harrison's faults, he had always tried to cushion the blow whenever he had something bad to tell her, as if he could somehow come across as an angel of mercy rather than the devil in disguise. Or perhaps the party caught in the middle of dire events, but not to be blamed for circumstances beyond his control.

Sitting up in bed, Emma suddenly felt more vulnerable than she had in all her life. She saw herself as a forty-five year old hag, with breasts that had begun to sag and hips that had expanded with each year and thighs that were beginning to resemble something akin to cauliflower. Ebony hair that was once full and vibrant had become listless and lifeless, and seemed determined to remain a convoluted salt and pepper no matter how many different dyes she applied to it. Crows feet had taken up permanent residence at the corners of her eyes, a rich café au lait, which had once been surrounded by taut, butterscotch skin that now seemed dull and tired.

She wondered if he saw her that way. Had she gotten too old for him, now that she had left behind the young gorgeous woman he once said he worshipped? Was she no longer enough for him now that he began to sense his own mortality at the age of forty-eight?

Had he really betrayed her in the worst way a husband could ever betray a wife?

He seemed to be reading her mind as he stared at her without blinking. He remained wedged inside the doorway, as if to come closer would only make what he had to say that much more difficult. His lips were in bunches and opened slightly as if trying to say words that wouldn't come out. She noted now the furrow ever deepening on his brow and couldn't help but think that he suddenly looked every bit his age and then some.

Finally, he stepped into their room and up to the

foot of the bed. He turned away, as if he could not stand the sight of her, before meeting her gaze head on.

"I said I'm involved with another woman."

This time there was no mistaking his meaning, Emma thought. He was having a <u>sexual</u> relationship with someone else. He had forsaken their marriage vows to be with someone, no doubt younger, sexier, able to bear his children, brainless.

Even then, painful as it was, she wanted to make him tell her in clear English what he meant.

And with whom he meant it.

I wouldn't want to make false assumptions.

She was wearing a silk and lace coral nightgown that he had given her for their twenty-fifth anniversary just this year. But she felt naked and humiliated, as if she had just been violated, and pulled the satin comforter up over her chest.

"I'm not a mind reader, Harrison," she spoke as nonchalantly as possible. *But I can read the guilt written all over your handsome face.* "What on earth are you talking about? You mean you're involved with a woman on yet another committee for dealing with substance abuse or illiteracy?" Aside from his writing, Harrison had practically made a career out of taking on various causes for making the world a better, kinder place to live in.

Now she wondered if, in reality, he had been thinking more about *his* own world in Elk Springs, Oregon, the coastal town they lived in where the laidback, outdoorsy life was much the same as it had been for over a century? Including apparently the keeper of shameful secrets that ultimately rose from the depths of the murky waters of the ocean to the surface where ripples threatened the façade of calmness.

His eyes hardened and lower lip quivered. "For heaven's sake, baby, don't make this anymore difficult than it already is."

She felt the bile rise from her throat. Glaring, she said, "If you expect me to make this easy for you, you're sorely mistaken." She could feel the rapid beat of her heart slamming against her chest like a drum. *Do I really want to hear what he has to say?* Might this all somehow seem like a bad dream, someone else's bad dream, if she refused to listen to any more?

But Emma knew she must listen. She wanted to — *had to* — hear all the gory details of his betrayal. It was the only way she could possibly come to terms with it. *And deal with him.*

Maybe it would be better if I shot him between the eyes? Emma considered seriously.

She had become an expert markswoman thanks to him and his damned fascination with guns. Big ones, little ones, and everything in between. She would make certain that the last thing he ever saw with those smug, deceiving eyes was the hatred he had created in her before she pulled the trigger.

Then, for good measure, she would shoot him

down there between his legs, where he had taken what was hers and given it to someone else.

Someone who had no right to him.

Someone who hadn't been through the ordeals, stresses, and strains he had put her through.

Someone who hadn't bankrolled his aspirations for years till they finally began to pay for themselves.

Someone who hadn't invested the years in a marriage that was supposed to be till <u>death</u> do them part.

She found him in the study that morning, having said he would wait for her there while she got dressed. She had not argued the point, having no desire to hear about his infidelity in the bedroom of all places.

Their bedroom.

Had *she* slept with him in there?

Did they make love in our bed?

Over and under *their* velvet blankets and silk charmeuse sheets?

Harrison had taken the liberty of fixing them both a brandy. Emma suspected that this was probably his third or fourth this morning. He wasn't a heavy drinker by and large. But that didn't stop him from indulging whenever it suited his fancy, usually to calm his nerves.

Or guilt.

She took the crystal goblet he extended to her,

but drank none. It was as if, coming from him she saw it as something akin to poison.

"I never planned for this to happen," Harrison uttered pathetically. "It just did."

Like hell it did. Nothing ever just happens, Emma thought, seething. It takes two selfish, sinful people to make it happen.

She flashed hateful eyes at one of them. "How long?" Emma heard herself say, as if this would somehow make a difference in the way she felt.

Had it been going on for years, without her ever suspecting?

Or had he decided practically overnight that having another lover was precisely what the doctor ordered to satisfy his overpowering sexual cravings? Or faltering sexual prowess?

Harrison put the goblet to his lips thoughtfully. "Is that really important?" he hesitated uncomfortably.

"*How long?*" Her voice rose threateningly. She needed to know just how long he had played her for a fool. How long he had abused her love and devotion to him. How long he had taken everything she had ever wanted in life and destroyed it in an instant.

"Six months," he said matter-of-factly.

Half a year.

One hundred and eighty-two days.

One hundred and eighty-two nights.

When he wasn't with her, he was with his

whore.

When *they* made love, which wasn't very often in the past six months, had he really been making love to *her?*

And what about when they weren't making love? Had he been sleeping with his mistress when Harrison claimed to be at his office or the cabin, writing?

Or when he was supposed to be on a book tour?

Or giving a lecture?

Or hunting?

Or flying that damned plane he loved to do as a hobby?

Had she been the first? Or the latest in a string of lovers?

Emma felt sick to her stomach. She bent over in pain, as if she had been on the receiving end of a George Foreman punch to the midsection. Harrison, feigning concern, put his hands on her.

"Are you all right?" His voice was thickly coated with sincerity. Or perhaps pity. She would accept neither. Whatever he was offering came too little, too late.

Of course, I'm not all right! What woman would be were she in my shoes?

She willed herself to put aside the nauseous feeling, straightening up, and slapping his hands away like they were on fire.

"Don't you touch me, you *bastard!*"

Harrison looked as if it was he who had been crushed, betrayed, and humiliated. "I know how you must feel." Even then he averted his face, realizing how hollow the words must have sounded.

Her eyes became razor slits. "You can't possibly know how I feel. How could you? I've given my life to you, Harrison. I've been *faithful* to you. I've allowed you to lead a life often separate from *our* life. All I ever asked in return was that you remain loyal to me, *in and out* of bed. But you took advantage of my love and naivety, and I hate you for it!"

Do I really? Emma had to ask herself.

Could she truly hate the only man she had ever loved, no matter what he did?

But how could she ever love him again, in spite of her feelings?

Her mouth felt dry, as if she had been in the desert for a month. She found herself lifting the brandy from the bar and drinking it, if only to wet her throat.

Though she wanted only to drown herself in sorrows, there were still other questions, other answers Emma needed to concern herself with. Because she'd had no experience with a cheating husband, she had not been prepared to face all the implications that came with the territory.

Why had he told her of his affair? To absolve his guilty conscience?

To cruelly hurt her in the worst way possible?

Or was it because he was planning to leave her for this other woman?

The mere notion sent a shiver up and down Emma's spine. Somehow, in her shock, she had not considered that it was he who might want to dump her rather than the other way around.

Was he even worth fighting for? she had to ask herself. Or should she be grateful that he had revealed his secret life, thereby making him worthless to her?

Maybe he was telling her this because the affair was now over and Harrison wanted her forgiveness. And to renew their love and commitment to one another.

Could their lives ever possibly be the same again? Or had his admission made trust a veritable impossibility from this day forward, no matter what else happened?

"Who is she?" Emma asked him pointblank, as if she needed to know this in order to put a face and body to this nightmare where there seemed no escape.

Her mind conjured up the possibilities.

Was it Karin Bremmer, Harrison's editor that he had been spending an increasing amount of time with in the last year? She was an attractive bottle-blonde, a few years younger than Emma, who couldn't seem to find enough reasons not to see Harrison.

How about Evangeline del Grenada, the best selling romance novelist who wore her hair in shimmering Senegalese twists and had a body to die for? At least Emma saw it that way. She was sure Harrison did as well during the time they spent together at book functions and supposedly chance meetings.

Or perhaps Lena Richardson, the thirtyish and vivacious organizer of the nonprofit group offering assistance to inner city children on the brink of delinquency? Against Emma's wishes, Harrison had insisted on volunteering his services in raising money and counseling youth on the pitfalls of running away, substance abuse, and antisocial behavior, though he himself had come from an upper middle-class, functional family and never saw the wrong side of the law. For this participation Lena Richardson was eternally grateful.

Then there was Samantha Warren, the newly widowed next-door neighbor. She was barely forty, gorgeous, lonely, well to do, and made no secret of her attraction to Harrison. He, of course, scoffed at the notion, insisting she meant nothing to him. But that didn't stop him from feeling obliged to assist her with household maintenance and landscaping projects at every opportunity now that she was left without a husband to perform these tasks. Or apparently the will to hire professional help. Especially with such a willing and available neighbor to come to her rescue like a black knight in shining armor.

Harrison hastily poured himself another drink, while seeming to get into her mind and understanding what she must have been thinking.

"It's not anyone you know," he said, as if she

should somehow applaud him for this consideration. "We met at a book signing earlier this year. We hit it off right away, like we were...."

He checked himself, as if the weight of his words were too haunting for even him to say.

"Meant for each other," Emma finished for him, what they both knew he had once felt about her.

He drank the brandy and, with wet lips, said with an apologetic tone, "She's quite young...in her early twenties. She's actually read everything I've ever written. Even those pieces that appeared in obscure magazines. I was amazed."

And obviously pleased with this ego-tripping worship of his young tart, Emma thought sickeningly. She too had once fed his ego until it had become more accommodating than honest.

Had this caused Harrison to look elsewhere for such attention? *Am I supposed to blame myself for neglecting him and leading into the arms of another woman?*

Harrison's eyes lighted as if he was floating on a cloud of energy. "She makes me feel young, alive, needed."

But I need you, Emma told herself. She had always needed him. Why couldn't he see and respect that?

When had he stopped needing her?

"Do you love her?" The very words played back in Emma's mind like a broken record. Asking them and waiting to hear the answer was like being strapped to the electric chair and waiting to see if there would be a last second reprieve or a violent, painful death by electrocution. Did she really want to hear his reply?

Could she stand it if he actually <u>loved</u> this girl toy who had caused him to forsake his marriage vows?

The thought of being unloved caused Emma greater anxiety than anything else. With the possible exception of loving a bastard who had torn her heart out.

In evading her question, Emma knew that Harrison had said everything she didn't want to hear loud and clear.

She should hack him up into little pieces.

And send his remains to his starry-eyed slut.

Along with the burned pages of his manuscripts.

Then the bitch would have his life's work in ashes to remember him by.

Or perhaps it would be more appropriate and painful if it was *he* who burned to death, Emma pondered, surprised by the wickedness of her thoughts. She could imagine pouring gasoline or cooking oil over him <u>and</u> his mistress while they were asleep, after making love. She would wake them so they could see the revulsion in her eyes, just before dropping the match.

Their inflamed bodies would light up like a

torch. Deathly, hideous screams would roar from their
mouths while the flesh tore from their limbs and nerve
endings sizzled excruciatingly. Soon they would be
reduced to charred bones and ashes.

All the while Emma would watch this horror
unfold, and curse Harrison for turning her into an
unforgiving beast who no longer cared about life,
living, and compassion.

"I hope we can still be friends," Harrison told
her as if he knew it was as unlikely as man traveling
to Mars and back in their lifetime.

He was putting clothes in a bag atop the bed two
days after telling Emma in effect that he was in love
with another woman. Even if the words failed to come
from his lips as if to do so might send her over the
edge.

The mere thought of it had done just that. She
had slapped him but Emma felt as if it was she who
had been hit harder than she could ever have
imagined. She had told him to get the hell out, hoping
that Harrison might somehow come to his senses, tell
her it was all a mistake, and beg her forgiveness.

But it was not to be.

He had left without so much as a meager
attempt at reconciliation, having clearly anticipated
such and made other plans for living arrangements.

Plans that no longer included Emma. Or her
wishes that they stay together as husband and wife.

"The moment you slept with another woman—if you can call it that," she had told him, "you ended any chance of us remaining friends. I have no intentions of going from your wife and lover to someone you think you can come to for comfort when your little bimbo decides you are too old, ugly, unsatisfying, and too much of an asshole for her."

Harrison had flung several pairs of designer slacks and knit boxer shorts into the bag, and hit Emma with a contorted glare. "Sorry you feel that way. I was truly hoping we could somehow end this more civilized."

"No you weren't," she challenged him. "You were hoping to get the *best* of all worlds, just like the characters in one of your damned novels. But it doesn't work that way in the real world. You made your uncivilized bed, Harrison. Now I hope you and your mistress drown in it!"

Emma found that it had become increasingly easier to vent her feelings to him and herself. She knew that she couldn't simply go away like the good wife who had been taken advantage of and mistreated. He didn't deserve to get off that lightly. She had worked too hard at making their marriage successful to watch it come apart at the seams and dismiss it as if simply swatting away a gnat.

There were no more words exchanged between them until Harrison had zipped his bag, grabbed it, and on the way out of their room, said colorlessly, "I'll pick up the rest of my things later. I'm sure we'll be able to work out a satisfactory arrangement on property settlement and the like." He paused, looking at her with perhaps a twinge of regret, but not enough to stay. "Goodbye, Emma."

She said nothing, wanting only to hear him leave, for she could no longer stand the sight or smell of him. When she heard the front door click shut, Emma knew that the world she had come to know and love had changed forever.

And for the worst.

She had sunk down to the maple hardwood floor, in the room Emma had once felt so comfortable in, and cried for the first time. The tears stung her cheeks like angry bees and seemed to embody all the feelings that raced through her like a locomotive out of control. She no longer had a husband. Or a lover. Or a confidant. Or a best friend.

Another woman had inherited the man she'd dedicated herself to in body and spirit.

But, instead of being engrossed with self-pity, Emma found herself absorbed with anger.

Loathing.

Discontent.

Revenge.

She wanted to kill him. Plain and simple.

It was the only way to free herself from the unbearable feelings of betrayal and anguish. And prevent him from taking what was hers and giving it to another woman unjustly.

Now, as she sat in the room where her life fell apart, Emma contemplated the many ways in which she could carry out the deed.

A single gunshot to the head.

Or maybe it would take several bullets to get the job done.

Carbon monoxide poisoning.

Strangulation.

Asphyxiation.

Electrocution.

Hanging.

Bludgeoning.

Running over with her car, again and again.

Castration.

That last thought clung to Emma like a second skin. She wondered how long it would take Harrison to bleed to death from the source of his abandonment and utter betrayal.

She wished death would not come too swiftly, for it would only be equitable to what she felt if he were forced to suffer for some time before the end came without mercy.

The woman sat impassively at the defense table beside her court-appointed attorney in the Elk Springs courthouse. She was on trial for the murder of her husband and attempted murder of his lover. He had been shot ten times at close range. His lover had been shot three times, miraculously surviving the assault, though left a paraplegic.

Across the room, the prosecutor fidgeted nervously at his table, glancing occasionally at the defendant.

The jury sat tensely, carefully avoiding looking directly at anyone, as if to do so might tip the scales one way or the other.

The judge took all this in, drew a sigh, and regarded the jury foreman. "Have you reached a verdict?"

Swallowing evenly, he said, "Yes, we have, Your Honor."

The verdict was passed from the bailiff to the judge, who glanced at it with no indication from her facial expression of what it read, before sending it in reverse order back to the jury foreman.

"Will the defendant please rise," the judge ordered.

Her attorney stood first, then urged her upward. The prosecutor joined them.

The judge knew this was the moment of truth when life and death hung in the balance like time standing still. She considered this with a sense of satisfaction for a moment or two before regarding the foreman.

"You may read the verdict."

The foreman licked his lips, refraining from eyeing the defendant, as if to do so would result in its own form of punishment. "We, the jury, find the defendant guilty of first degree murder and attempted murder."

Judge Emma Kincaid quickly restored order to the court and immediately directed that the newly convicted be remanded to the county jail to await sentencing.

Emma gazed down at the attractive woman as she was being led away by sheriff's deputies. For a moment their eyes met, and Emma felt empathy that she could never express to the woman. Or, for that matter, anyone else.

In the courtroom she was a judge, sworn to uphold the law to the best of her ability.

In her private life, she was a female on the brink of insanity. One who had all the frailties, weaknesses, and vulnerabilities of a woman scorned.

A woman who no longer cared to uphold laws with respect to her own marriage. Or what was left of it.

Emma departed the courthouse a short while later and went directly home. She was still thinking about the case she had just presided over and its ironies when she pulled up to her driveway. Waiting there beside a dark sedan were two tall men dressed in cheap suits. By their demeanor and respectful but uneasy expressions, Emma knew instinctively they were police detectives. After all, she had seen enough of them show up in her courtroom. What she didn't know was why they were at her house.

Could they possibly read my mind? Know what

I'm planning, only to arrest before the crime?

She stepped out of her car, a silver Lexus Coupe. They approached her.

"Judge Kincaid," said the older of the two, removing his police identification from his pocket, "I'm Detective Bochco and this is Detective Jefferson. We need to talk to you."

Emma lifted a brow, perspiration building beneath her white polka dot skirt suit.

"May I ask what this is all about?" She tried to keep her voice curious but calm.

The detectives looked at each other, as if carrying a great secret.

Detective Jefferson, an African-American, scratched hair bumps on his chin and said tonelessly, "Mind if we go inside?"

I would just as soon hear what you have to say out here, thank you, she thought warily.

"Has something happened to my husband?" It seemed a perfectly natural question to Emma for some reason. Hardly indicated she had some sixth sense.

Again the detectives exchanged glances and frowns as though she were onto something.

Emma's heart skipped a beat. "Something has happened to him. Has Harrison been in an accident?" She wasn't sure why she chose to use the word "accident" instead of say, "heart attack," victim of a crime, or some other reference to death or dismemberment.

Detective Bochco's look was grim, and he said, "There was a plane crash, a twin engine Cessna. It went down in the Cascade Mountains. There were two people on board, Harrison Kincaid, and a young woman who hasn't been identified yet." He gulped, and his face turned beet red. "I'm afraid that neither one survived."

Like the good wife, Emma flushed and began to wail like a newborn baby. "No-o-o-o," she cried out. "There must be some mistake!"

She knew there was no mistake. Harrison had told her he and his mistress were going to the cabin to *chill out* for a couple of days. He always took a rented plane up there, preferring the air to the narrow, often perilous mountain roads.

Obviously he never made it.

Or *they* never did.

When she finally got rid of the detectives a half-hour later, Emma felt sorely in need of a drink. She went to the study and filled a wineglass with brandy, before retreating to her sanctuary — the bedroom she once shared with her husband. She was in disbelief over the turn of events. It was almost as if she had willed the accident to happen.

And yes, it had been an *accident*, she mused, hilarious as it sounded.

Emma had never even considered Harrison's death by plane crash, though somehow it seemed fitting. She imagined the terror he and his ill-fated lover must have felt as the plane was spiraling out of control, knowing that death was imminent ... mere seconds away, that seemed like years.

She wondered if Harrison had thought of her just before the moment of impact.

Had he considered that the circumstances that would result in his tragic death might never have occurred were it not for his own misguided choices?

If not, maybe you should have, sweetheart.

Emma sat on the antique brass bed and sipped on the brandy, while laughing hysterically. "To my darling late husband. May you and your whore rot in the hell of your own making."

She tasted a bit more of the brandy and thought about how justice seemed to have a way of prevailing when all was said and done.

How deliciously sweet it was, she thought.

Emma suddenly felt a tightening in her stomach and lightheaded. Then her throat felt as if it was on fire.

What was happening to her?

She stood up so swiftly that the brandy went flying and the glass fell from her hand onto the floor, shattering into a thousand pieces.

Clutching her throat, Emma felt as if a foreign enemy was invading her entire body like cancer. One determined to make sure she did not survive. But not before seeing that she suffered horribly.

She fell backward, her body wracked with pain, before she hit the floor with a thud. Her voice rasped, but she was unable to scream.

As she lay on the bedroom floor, eyes fixed on the mahogany entryway, Emma envisioned Harrison's face. His chilling gaze was looking down at her with satisfaction. So consumed with his death, she had forgotten when pouring the brandy that it had been laced with strychnine intended for her husband as a fitting and undeniable end to their journey.

STORY TWELVE

A DESOLATE DEATH

by Cindy Daniel

As he approached the turnoff to Jon and Debby's house, the short hairs at the base of Matt Robins' neck bristled. Desolate roads had a way of doing that to even the bravest of men. Something about turning off a main road and plunging into an abyss. Black fog enveloping your vehicle. Dense, moist air filling your lungs.

This was commonplace on country byways. But, for some reason he couldn't explain, it was unsettling on this particular evening. Their plans for a wild night of gambling and drinking didn't include the ache developing in his gut and the sweat on his brow.

Matt had driven this stretch of road hundreds of times. Dusk and dawn. Drunk and sober. Why was he getting so spooked this evening? Was he turning into a pussy?

In an effort to break out of the funk, he decided to think about something that always brought a smile to his face. His wife Evvie. She always said the silliest things. In fact, earlier today she had been poking fun at him and his giddiness.

"Okay, Hon. You boys enjoy your men's night out. Heaven forbid we women try to keep a bunch of overworked and overwrought boys from their male bonding rituals."

Just remembering her heart-shaped face and the pucker of her delicate lips making that declaration, only to end it with a deep throated belch, cracked him up. He laughed out-loud, breaking the stillness in his Jeep.

That's why he loved Evvie. Tiny, petite little thing who wasn't afraid to act any way she wanted. He couldn't wait to tell the guys about this. The guys were crazy over Evvie. Her spontaneity. Sense of humor. And how she accepted everyone just as they were.

The first time the guys met her was a couple years ago as she breezed into the den, walking in front of the TV during the Super Bowl, scratching her crotch with one hand and crushing a beer can against her forehead with the other. She was a big hit. They loved her! Jealous that their wives were too prim and proper to do something like burp, fart, or scratch themselves. Always worried about social standing and political correctness, even in a town like Desolate.

In fact, they were only afforded the luxury of this Saturday poker night because Debby had left Wednesday morning on another week-long sabbatical giving Jon the rule of the roost. It's not that she wouldn't have approved of their behavior—she wouldn't have, but never had dared go against Jon's wishes—it's just that the guys didn't feel comfortable with her there while they partied.

This Saturday belonged to them, though. They had a place in the country to hide out. A chance to be the cowboys they believed they were: gun racks in their trucks, Stetson's in the seat of their brand new Hummers, and a keg of Lone Star in the backseat of their Jeeps ready to be chugged by whatever crazy new way they dreamed up. Away from the women folk.

Not to say the other women weren't good wives. Because Matt believed all his buddies were pretty lucky. Had women they loved, who loved them in return.

Joe's wife Caren was a lawyer. Elegant and chic. She was a great provider. Which allowed Joe the privilege (he called it responsibility) to stay home and play Mr. Mom to their rambunctious two-year-old. Wow, that was the life.

Then there was Tommy. The stray mutt of the pack. He was the only one that broke the mold and headed out of Desolate, Texas right after high school.

Desolate. A place where everyone knew your business, everyone got in your business, and everyone told your business (at least their version of it). Tommy always dreamed about the life outside his country bumpkin hometown. A life where you could live however you wanted, no apologies, no excuses. Not that Desolate was so bad. It was like all the other small towns across America, perfect on the outside, but rotten to the core. At least that's what he thought until he spent time in the real world. A world full of nameless faces, hard hearts, and mere acquaintances, but no friends.

Course, it wasn't until he ran out of money, and out of women to support him, that he made his realizations. Then he found his roots real quick. Well, he found his momma's house, that is. He was a pretty lucky old coot, his old high school sweetheart taking him back. Melody was a good woman. Said she couldn't resist his James Dean act, and he just needed a good woman to settle him down. Mel did a good job. Got him a position at the newspaper and kept his butt in church every Sunday.

And, of course, Jon had Debby who, even though she was pretty wrapped up with her Peace Corps trips, whatever that entailed, always left prepared meals in the freezer so he wouldn't go hungry in her absence. Casseroles, hamburgers, or fried chicken. Yes, Debby was the perfect Desolate wife, didn't work out of the house but kept a spotless home and a hot meal on the table. Involved in many charitable associations for the church. Catered to Jon more than a man like him deserved.

And when she wasn't around—well, they didn't want to know who took care of the insatiable sexual appetite Jon bragged about. He certainly said Debby was never able to satisfy it. The guys insisted they had a 'don't ask-don't tell' policy. However, when Jon decided to brag about a couple of conquests he'd made while the cat was away—the guys always listened. Policy or no policy.

But that wild lifestyle was lived vicariously through Jon. The others, they were all happy with what life had dealt them.

Matt's thoughts were disturbed by the scream of an errant night hawk on the prowl. Sounds of the Michelin tires crushing the pea gravel as he turned into Jon's secluded drive somehow drowned out the country crooner on the portable CD player resting on the bucket seat. Absence of lights from Jon and Debby's front windows added to the uneasiness he had felt earlier, and it didn't help that the Jeep headlights reflecting off the bumper of Jon's beat-up '63 Ford unibody provided the *only* illumination at this remote homestead.

He wasn't really surprised he had beat the other guys there. They usually straggled behind unless their wives were lighting a fire under them. But the fact there were no lights burning bothered Matt. Bothered him real bad. After all, Jon was expecting company. Most times he'd have the citronella torches blazing to keep the mosquitoes away from the front door, the electric blue of his fly-zapper casting a psychedelic glow from the back of the house. This time—nothing.

Second guessing himself, he began to wonder if maybe the gathering was tomorrow. Or, with Deb being gone all week, Jon had probably just been working and drinking, and forgot about sticking to any kind of real schedule anyway. Surely that was it. Yeah, he should've called Jon to firm things up. Now when *was* the last time they spoke? Wednesday, Thursday? Hell, Jon probably forgot all about the guys and took off to Lake Fork for a bass tournament.

Yeah, that was probably it. The fish were spawning and the guys probably never gave Saturday night another thought. It had happened before. Them forgetting to tell Matt. They never intentionally forgot him, but it pissed him off nonetheless. Tommy probably called Joe, who called Jon, who grabbed his cooler and headed to Fork without even remembering it was his duty to call Matt. Jon could be a real asshole like that.

If all those things made so much sense, why was Matt shifting into neutral and pulling the parking brake? He should just head straight to the boat ramp and look for the idiots making the most commotion. But before he had time to think about turning tail and leaving Desolate in his rearview mirror, the spotlights of Tommy's monster truck drew a beam on him.

No turning back now, he shoved his keys in his pocket, slammed the door, and walked to greet the twosome, the short hairs once again on end. The winds howled through the mesquite, and Matt sensed something foul blowing in the Desolate night. Suddenly he was glad Tommy had picked up Joe on the way over—something about strength in numbers, and he had a hunch they would need all the strength they could muster.

"What the hell?" Joe asked. "Jon get a better offer and decide to blow us off?"

Matt pointed to the Ford and said, "Unless the better offer came and picked him up, he's here somewhere."

Tommy laughed. "Heck guys, we could be walking in on coitus interruptus."

"Not like it's stopped us before," Joe replied, as he headed up the drive.

For Matt, stepping across the once familiar front deck seemed liked an eternity, when in fact it was only ten feet. Then came the monotonous ritual of staring each other down in an effort to receive a volunteer to be the first one through the door.

"Screw it." Matt said in resignation as his right hand pushed open the unlocked door, then found the light switch.

Every thing looked okay. Better than okay when you considered Jon had been batchin' it. Only a couple empty Shiner cans left crumpled atop the bar, which separated the living room from the kitchen. They could've done without the smell though. Jon had a habit of leaving the trash in the pantry until it was past ripe.

"Oooh whee." Joe said. "Surely he would've lit some candles to cover that up, if he was trying to have a love-fest."

"Hey, dick head," Tommy yelled. "We didn't come all the way to Bumfuk to play hide and seek."

While Tommy was shouting and heading toward the toilet, no doubt to drain the six pack he'd downed on the way over, Matt made his way around the bar.

"He's out here, guys," Matt explained, when he noticed the backdoor slightly cracked. "Hey dude, what's happening...." His question left hanging in the damp Desolate night.

Through the darkness Matt saw the still form of his friend. He approached him slowly, unsure of what to do, finally reaching for Jon's outstretched arm to see if there was life. "My God," he whispered.

"Drunk again, Bubba?" Tommy yelled, as he and Joe made their way out back. Matt stood, calmly feeling his way to another switch, and turned the porch light on, sending varmints scampering away from the house, back into the woods where they came from.

Joe sank to his knees, knowing he would be unable to stand much longer. Tommy looked to Matt who shook his head, confirming their unspoken question.

When he was sure he could find his voice, Matt called for help. He had always been the one to take charge. Tommy hadn't stopped puking, but luckily Joe pushed him toward the railing, directing his eruptions into the yard.

None of the guys were experts on dead people, but they knew a thing or two about dead animals, being as this was Texas and they all owned guns. By looking at Jon, and the amount of flies covering his carcass, their friend's last beer had been at least a day ago. Of course, this was a perverse line of thinking, but standing on a porch in the middle of Desolate, Texas with your friend bug-eyed and blue, well hell, what else was there to think about?

Things wouldn't happen fast, they never did in Desolate. It would take time for the law to arrive, so the guys went out front, putting a little distance between them and their friend. Joe walked over to Matt's Jeep and tapped the keg, figuring Tommy needed to rehydrate himself. A little brew would be good for him and Matt too.

Matt sat on the opened tailgate and gazed across the Desolate sky. Memories filled his head.

He was there when Jon and Debby walked out
on the rough parcel, anxious to build a life in the
country. Well, Debby wasn't that excited, but she
always did what Jon wanted. Never complained—even
when Jon would talk about their most intimate
moments, knowing it embarrassed her no end. She'd
sit quietly by his side as he mocked her commitment to
church, her efforts at being a good person. He'd brag
about his desires for wild sex and a hedonistic lifestyle
while sarcastically detailing the frigid affection she
offered, not caring about the tears of shame held in her
eyes.

Matt wondered how a sweet girl like Debby ever
got hooked up with Jon. But Evvie had always told
him love was blind. Debby only saw the good parts of
her husband. "And, face it," she'd tell Matt, "Desolate
didn't have a lot to offer her."

Matt was glad Debby didn't have to see Jon like
this. It might be more than she could handle.

Evvie insisted Matt bring the guys back to their
house. After spending the last few hours with the
sheriff going over every aspect of Jon and Debby's life,
Evvie figured the boys would need comfort food. She'd
also called their wives to let them know the events of
the evening and issued her invitation to them as well.
After all, it was a time you needed your friends around
you.

As she waited for everyone to arrive, she tried to
make some kind of sense of what Matt had told her.
Jon just sitting at his plastic patio table, face-down in

a bag of Fritos. Nothing else around except a paper plate, a piece of wadded up tin foil, and a few unopened Shiner's in the Styrofoam cooler. Must've just finished off his last meal. No doubt something Deb had cooked for him.

Sheriff said it appeared to be a heart attack, come on so fast he couldn't get help out there. Course, it could be true, Evvie decided. But, other than the silly food allergies they always teased him about, she thought Jon had always been pretty healthy. Healthy enough to test-drive every Desolate young lady, and some not so young, whenever Deb was out of town, Evvie thought with disgust.

"So, has anyone called Deb?" Evvie asked.

No one appeared to have the answer. They just sat around drinking their long-necks and throwing Chex mix into their mouths, keeping their hands busy and their minds numb.

Caren, who had asked for a frosted mug to pour her beer into, finally spoke. "Sheriff Miller said he'd try to call the Peace Corps, and see if they could locate her. But it may take a little time."

"Before we left their place," Matt offered, " A few of the deputies were going through papers to see if they could find phone numbers, contacts, that kinda thing. It wasn't looking good though."

Evvie walked over, put an arm around her husband's shoulder, and kissed the top of his head. Her heart ached for the pain Matt must be feeling.

Actually, thanks to the beer, Matt wasn't feeling

much pain. He was only thinking about how lucky he was to have his wife right beside him. A good woman. Always thinking of others. Like having a frosted mug on hand to offer the pretentious lawyer. Always making their Chex mix without peanuts because of Jon's allergy. Jon. Poor bastard.

"Funny," Melody said, "I never thought he'd go like that."

Caren, looking slightly appalled, asked, "How exactly did you think he'd go?"

Melody was a common girl. She didn't think twice about the look the lawyer was giving her. "Well, hell's bells Caren," Mel said, "everyone thought some irate husband would put a bullet through his skull."

"In his skull," Tommy added, "or in his nuts."

Any plans they'd had for a nice Sunday afternoon had been shot to heck. News traveled fast in Desolate, Texas and everyone had called Matt for a first-hand account. Finally things calmed, and Evvie was enjoying a glass of after-dinner wine.

"Sheriff Miller tells me they haven't had any luck reaching Deb," Evvie told Matt. "She's usually only gone on these trips for a week, so she may be home tomorrow." She grimaced, thinking about what awful news awaited.

"Doc says he's sure his heart just gave out on him," Evvie added. "A lifestyle of eating bad, drinking heavy, and playing hard, just did him in." Matt shook his head, thinking how his own habits resembled Jon's, with the exception of the wild women.

"You know, I guess I never considered we might be walking time bombs," Matt argued. "We're young strong men, for Chrissakes."

Evvie smiled the crooked grin that gave Matt comfort. "Hon," she said, "there wasn't evidence of anything else. You said it yourself."

"I know, I know. No foul play. Just him sitting on the back porch all by his lonesome. Not another soul around for miles."

Matt's steps sounded slow and heavy against the tile as he walked to the box on the drain board and poured a glass of wine for himself. "Evvie, I just keep thinking about how Jon must've felt. The pain he must've endured. Taking his last breath. All alone."

"I know Hon," she replied. "His wife off in another country. And all his wild women at home with their own families."

"Maybe he wasn't alone." Matt said, under his breath.

"She's been gone for two weeks now," Joe said, as he once again joined his friends around Matt and Evvie's table.

"The body'll keep." Matt assured them. "Old man Cieszinski's got him in cold storage."

"Tommy said the varmints got him pretty good." Melody never was one to mince words. Of course everyone gave Tommy the evil eye, wondering why in the world he'd mentioned that to his wife.

Evvie pushed back her chair, quietly walked down the hall, and returned in a few moments with a decorated hatbox. All eyes were on her.

"I went out to Desolate yesterday," Evvie explained. "This was in Debby's sewing room, tucked away behind her Bible study papers." She held the box tight against her chest, as if it held untold secrets. "I found some old calendars, those Hallmark purse-sized ones."

Matt knew she was stalling, searching for the right way to break the news. He offered her a smile of encouragement.

"Well," she said, "there were some phone numbers."

Basking under a Caribbean sun, Rum punch in hand, she slowly repositioned herself on the mahogany lounger. Spending lazy days aboard Tex's sailboat, *Peace Core*, riding turquoise waves, and casting her cares upon the water, was habit forming.

Tex, a philanthropist she'd met during one of her volunteer efforts — now her lover, her soul mate — was a vibrant, handsome man. He'd swept her off her feet and carried her away from the life she had settled for, the affairs and humiliation. She had taken control of her life. She had ended the cycle of abuse, and Desolate was behind her. And she knew the only other woman she would ever have to share Tex with was temptress of the deep.

Debby grinned as Tex lowered himself onto the adjoining lounger.

"It's good to see your pretty face all lit up," he said. "Didn't know if you'd ever be able to smile again."

"I can't remember when I've been so happy," she replied.

"So, do you think he ate...."

Deb raised her longs fingers, reached up, and covered Tex's mouth. "I think he came home, grabbed a beer, zapped the burgers I left for him, and started wondering which floozy he'd spend the night with." Her statement deliberate, without malice.

"So, you still hungry?" she asked as she walked to the drain-board and poured peanut oil into the pan. Her own stomach growling as she picked the burgers off the foil and tossed them onto the sizzling grill. Thoughts of Jon hadn't ruined her appetite.

When the cell-phone rang, the tinny sound seemed to echo across the rolling waves. She had known it would only be a matter of time. But she didn't expect it would be Evvie's voice.

"Deb, we've been trying to reach you for a couple weeks." Evvie's words came across the ocean clean and crisp. "It's about Jon."

But, before Evvie could deliver the news, Debby simply said, "I know." Then cast the phone across the starboard deck into the ocean spray.

About the Authors

J.K. Cummins is the author of Death Rides at Ascot, Shadowed by Evil, Awake from Evil Dreams and more than a hundred shorter works. Her crime fiction has appeared in Murder between Knife and Fork (German and French editions), Futures Mystery Anthology, Mystery Time, FAME, Dime, City Crimes: Country Crimes, Fedora IV, Maelstrom I (UK), and several other publications.

An active member of Mystery Writers of America and Sisters in Crime, she has received numerous writing awards for both novels and short stories. She currently teaches English at Palomar College in San Diego but spent twenty years living abroad, during which time she owned a travel business specializing in tours to the Middle East. She and her British husband still enjoy traveling extensively.

J.M.M. Holloway is a fifth-generation Texan, who recently returned to her home state after a twenty-year sojourn on the San Mateo Coast of California. Both locales color her short fiction, which has appeared in various e-zines and the print anthology Mystery in Mind.

Her story, "How to Kill a Peanut Queen," was inspired by the infamous Sweet Potato of Queens of Hunt Texas, although the two groups have only flamboyance in common.

J lives in the Texas Hill Country with her husband Bob, a research chemist turned university professor.

Kadi Easley is a mystery writer from Fulton, Missouri. Her work has appeared in Futures Mysterious Anthology Magazine and on various E-zines. Her recent story, Diamonds are Forever, was submitted to the 2005 Edgar committee.

She writes and works throughout the United States and parks in Missouri periodically to catch up with her two grown sons. If you'd like to see more of Kadi's work, stop by www.kadieasley.com

Megan Powell lives in suburban Philadelphia and sometimes vacations in the Adirondacks. She has never needed to hide a body or cover up a murder, but planning for such eventualities has provided her with hours of entertainment. Sometimes her husband assists with said plans, which bodes well for the future of the relationship.

Megan's most recent anthology, *Crossings*, was published in 2004 and her novel *Waxing* is due for release in 2005. Her short fiction has appeared in various magazines and anthologies. She putters online with the webzines *Shred of Evidence* and *Fables*, as well as a homepage at www.meganpowell.net.

Pam McWilliams got hooked on Nancy Drew as a young girl and never stopped reading. She graduated to Agatha Christie, P.D. James, and the wider world of great literature, but mystery – her first love – remains her passion and became her writer's muse. Lots of living happened first.

She chose business writing initially because she thought she lacked imagination. These days she's bombarded by story ideas every time she picks up the newspaper, waits in a carpool line, or sits in the stands at a football game.

After working briefly as a feature writer for a small town paper, she moved to Manhattan to spend a decade in the business world – writing, posturing, traveling. One day she got talked into a sales job at a Wall Street brokerage firm. Temperamentally she was unsuited to work on a trading floor, but she remembers the insanity, the greed, the giant personalities - it was there that she discovered the simple joy of observing other people. She married and had two children, and one day she woke up with a big imagination.

She started to write fiction and couldn't stop. Today as she adds to her eclectic collection of short stories, works on her contemporary young adult mystery series (an ode to Nancy Drew), and fleshes out the plot of her first adult mystery novel, she wonders, is one lifetime enough? www.pdmcwilliams-pdqmedia.com.

Roberta Rogow is the author of four mystery novels in which Mr. Charles Lutwidge Dodgson(better known as Lewis Carroll) teams up with young Dr. Arthur Conan Doyle to solve mysterious deaths when the local police either cannot, do not, or will not take action.

She has also written Sherlock Holmes pastiche stories and participated in the "Merovingen Nights" Shared Universe anthologies.

When she is not writing or attending Science Fiction and Mystery conventions, Roberta is a children's librarian at a public library in New Jersey.

Heather Hiestand's first short story, Nancy's

Magic Penny, was written when she was seven. Though the story was popular in grade school publishing circles, it took her years to find additional publication for her short fiction. Now she looks forward to finding publication for her novels.

She resides in Washington State where she owns a small business that provides non-medical services for seniors and the disabled. You can reach her at HAHiestand@aol.com.

Gesine Schulz is the author of the popular German children's mystery series, *Privatdetektivin Billie Pinkernell* about a spunky girl detective. In her series of crime stories for adults she writes about the (not always clean) cases of Karo Rutkowsky, owner of a struggling detective agency and sought-after cleaning lady. One of these stories, "The Panama Hen", was included in "The World's Finest Mystery and Crime Stories, Fourth Annual Collection", 2003, edited by Ed Gorman and Martin H. Greenberg.

A librarian by training, Gesine Schulz spent more than a decade living and working abroad. Mostly in New York, but also in South America, Ireland and Switzerland. Nowadays she divides her time between Essen/Germany and her garden in West Cork/Ireland.

He is a member of Sisters in Crime as well as the Internet Chapter, and the German Chapter 'Moerderische Schwestern' (www.sinc.de) Gesine is currently working on new Karo-stories, her next children's mystery and is planning a crime novel. www.gesineschulz.com   www.billie-pinkernell.de

Gunhild Muschenheim, translator for Gesine

Schulz, was born in Germany, and has spent most of her life in the States. She has a translator's certificate from New York University. After some years in London she and her husband now live in the South-West of Ireland.

Paul D. Marks is the *stealth screenwriter*, making his living from optioning screenplays of his own and rewriting (script doctoring) other people's scripts and developing their ideas. He has also had short stories appear in the "Dime," "Murder on Sunset Boulevard," "Murder by Thirteen" and "Fiction on the Run" anthologies, as well as in such magazines as "Crimestalker Casebook," "Futures" and others. His story *Netiquette* won first place in the Futures Short Story Contest. *Dem Bones* was a finalist in the Southern Writers Association contest.

Paul's noir novel *White Heat* was recently announced as a winner in the 2005 Southwest Writers Contest. He also recently signed with a New York Agent to represent that novel. *White Heat* is a detective thriller about a private eye in LA trying to redeem himself in a time of racial turmoil—the LA riots of 1992—by finding a killer—a killer he unwittingly aided. Paul is currently working on another mystery-thriller as well as a mainstream novel.

Besides fiction and screen work, Paul has sold non-fiction articles to the Los Angeles Daily News, The Los Angeles Times, The Los Angeles Herald Examiner, and American Premiere magazine. He was also a contributing editor on The Hollywood Gazette.

Paul has also lectured on writing and screen

writing at UCLA, California State University, San Bernardino, Learning Tree University and other seminars or conferences.

Good Old Days is the second story to appear in print featuring Paul's character Bobby Saxon.

A Los Angeles native, Paul loves the city that L.A. was. Dodging bullets, he's not so sure about the city it is today. You can find him at www.PaulDMarks.com.

Patricia Gulley is a retired travel agent from a major travel agency in the USA. She has, and still, travels widely, cruising is her favorite. She grew up in Pennsylvania and worked with two airlines in New York City before moving to Portland Oregon, where she now lives on a floating home. Though she never found a body, though one night half a smashed pumpkin stuck between her house and the walkway gave her a scare, she has experienced almost everything else mentioned in her story. She loves clubs, conferences and conventions and has helped run a few for Mystery and Science Fiction. She is the editor of the In SinC Docket. She has one daughter and two grandchildren.

R. Barri Flowers is a prolific writer, living in the Pacific Northwest. A fan of mystery, thriller, and romantic suspense fiction, he has a long background in criminology and has used this to write both nonfiction and fiction books.

The author of more than thirty books, his nonfiction titles include the best selling true crime book now in its seventh printing, *The Sex Slave Murders* (St. Martin's Press, 1996), as well as *Murders*

In The United States (McFarland, 2004), *Male Crime And Deviance* (Charles C Thomas, 2003, *Murder, At The End Of The Day And Night* (Charles C Thomas, 2002, *Kids Who Commit Adult Crimes* (Haworth, 2002), *Domestic Crimes, Family Violence And Child Abuse* (McFarland, 2000), *Drugs, Alcohol And Criminality In American Society* (McFarland, 1999), and *Female Crime, Criminals And Cellmates* (McFarland, 1995).

Fiction by Flowers includes the bestselling legal thrillers, *Persuasive Evidence* (Dorchester, 2004) and *Justice Served* (Dorchester, 2005). Look for his next powerful legal thriller from Dorchester, *State's Evidence*, to hit the bookstore shelves in 2006.

R. Barri Flowers is a longtime member of Sisters in Crime, Romance Writers of America, Mystery Writers of America, American Crime Writers League, American Society of Criminology, and Kiss of Death.

When not writing, he enjoys traveling (often to scope out new locations for his thrillers) across the country and abroad; listening to jazz standards, watching basketball, football, and baseball; classic movies, tennis, walking, dancing, museums, and playing on the computer.

Visit the author's website at: http://rbarriflowers.homestead.com

Cindy Daniel lives in Rockwall, Texas (a lakeside suburb of Dallas) with her husband. She works as an orthopedic research coordinator at a Dallas area children's hospital.

Cindy is the Southwest Chapter President of Mystery Writers of America and was the 2004 President of Sisters in Crime - Internet Chapter. She is a member of Mystery Writers of America, Sisters in Crime, SinC Internet Chapter, SinC Guppies, Romance Writers of America - Kiss of Death, and American Medical Writers Association; she is the Dallas Meeting Coordinator for the Southwest Chapter of Mystery Writers of America.

Cindy's debut novel, *Death Warmed Over*, was released in hardcover in October 2003 and paperback in April 2005. The series is set in the East Texas Bible belt and is packed with sibling rivalry, lust, old-fashioned Christian guilt, death of a beauty queen, and, of course, pickup trucks.

The second of the series, *A Family Affair*, was released hardcover in September 2005. Return to Destiny, Texas - where the eccentric heirs, animal activists and stray bullets threaten to spoil Hannah's romance. Good thing the Sheriff of Van Zandt County has a big gun!

"What Janet Evanovich does for the Jersey burbs, Cindy Daniel takes to the back streets of the Bible Belt in a rollicking, Texas-sized mystery!" *Ann Cavan, Sisters In Crime*

In her spare time, Cindy is writing a non-fiction account of her breast cancer experience — *It's Not About You: A Mother and Daughter's Journey Through Cancer.*

Please visit cindy at her website: www.deathwarmedovermysteries.com

SISTERS IN CRIME – INTERNET CHAPTER

All royalties from the sale of this anthology are being donated to the Internet Chapter of Sisters in Crime.

Sisters in Crime is an international organization of readers and writers dedicated to raising awareness of women's contributions to the mystery genre. The organization was founded in 1986 by Sara Paretsky and other women mystery writers and enthusiasts and now has over 50 chapters around the world.

The *Internet Chapter* of Sisters in Crime was founded in 1994 to provide a convenient meeting ground for members of SinC who live in places where there are no local chapters. Our purpose: to maintain a chapter accessible to everyone who has a computer and a modem.

Is SinC just for women? Not at all. Men who want to see that women authors get a fair deal in the mystery field are more than welcome. We cherish our male "sisters."

All members of SinC are welcome, whether they belong to a local chapter or not. Join with us. Share in the uniqueness of being the only Sisters in Crime chapter which meets exclusively on the Internet. For more information – visit us at www.sinc-ic.org

MURDER ON SUNSET BOULEVARD

SISTERS IN CRIME * LA CHAPTER

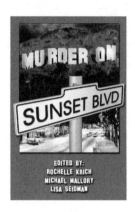

November 2002, $12.95

ISBN 1-929976-19-4 Trade Paperback

From the Los Angeles Chapter of Sisters in Crime, *Murder on Sunset Boulevard*, Edited by Rochelle Krich (Jessica Drake series), Michael Mallory (The Second Mrs. Watson series) and Lisa Seidman (professional TV writer), the book features 12 stories set along the famed thoroughfare from the gritty streets of downtown to the palatial homes of Malibu Beach.

Contributors: Dana Kouba, Gayle McGary, Richard Partlow, Dale Furutani, Joan Waites, Kate Thornton, Gay Toltl Kinman, Mae Woods, Linda O. Johnston, Paul D. Marks, Anne Riffenburgh, Gabriella Diamond.